I0535905

# Twelve Days of Christmas

## HER SIDE OF THE STORY - BOOK ONE

EMMA LEA

Copyright © 2025 by Emma Lea

All rights reserved.

No part of this book may be reproduced in any form or by any electronic or mechanical means, including information storage and retrieval systems, without written permission from the author, except for the use of brief quotations in a book review.

Cover design by Michelle Birrell

Book design and production by Michelle Birrell

Images licensed by Adobe Stock

 Formatted with Vellum

# Other books by Emma Lea

This is Emma Lea's complete book library at time of publication, but more books are coming out all the time. Find out every time Emma releases a book by going to her website (www.emmaleaauthor.com) and signing up for her newsletter.

## SWEET ROMANCES

These are romantic tales without the bedroom scenes and the swearing, but that doesn't mean they're boring!

### *The Young Royals*

A Royal Engagement

Lord Darkly

A Royal Entanglement

A Royal Entrapment

A Royal Expectation

A Royal Elopement

A Royal Embarrassment

A Very Royal Christmas

A Royal Enticement

### *The Kabiero Royals*

Royal Ruse

Royal Refinement

Royal Holiday

### *Bookish Book Club Novellas*

Meeting Prince Charming

Meeting the Wizard of Oz

Meeting Santa Claus

## SWEET & SEXY ROMANCES

In my Sweet & Sexy Romances I turn up the heat with a little bit of sexy. No swearing, or very minimal swearing, and brief, tasteful and not too graphic bedroom scenes.

### *Love, Money & Shoes Series*

Walk of Shame

### *Standalone Novels*

Amnesia

### *The Trouble With Series*

(Co-Authored with Kirsty McManus)

The Trouble with Falling

The Trouble with Fame

The Trouble with Forever

## COSY ROMANCES WITH A HINT OF SPICE

What is a cosy romance with a hint of spice?

Think Pumpkin Spice Latte...Warm and sweet and delicious with just a hint of spice to tantalise.

### *All in Good Time Series*

Just a Matter of Time

That One Time

It's About Time

Over Time

In Our Own Time

## HOT & SEXY ROMANCES

Hot & Spicy Romances turn the heat way up. They contain swearing and sexy scenes and the characters get hot under the collar.

Recommended for 18+ readers

### *Brisbane City Hearts (formerly TGIF)*

Love to Hate You

Want to Date You

Hate to Want You

### *Collins Bay Series*

Last Call

The Christmas Stand-Off

### *Standalone Novels*

Learning to Breathe

The Wedding Pact

The Blind Date

### *Romantic Suspense*

Hide & Seek

## TOO HOT TO HANDLE ROMANCES

These are definitely 18+ reads and contain graphic sex scenes and high-level swearing—not for the faint of heart

### *The Young Billionaires*

The Billionaire Stepbrother

The Billionaire Daddy

The Billionaire Muse

The Billionaire Replacement

The Billionaire Trap

Christmas with the Billionaire

### *Music & Lyrics*

Rock Star

Songbird

Strings

Sticks

Symphony

### *The Playbook Series*

In Like Flynn

Manscaping

Game Changer

Scandal

Final Notice

### *Serendipity Trilogy*

The Wrong Girl

### *Hope Springs*

Unbreak My Heart

Untangle My Heart

Unravel My Heart

Unwrap My Heart

### Romantasy

Romantasy books have a touch of magic to go along with the romance –
Romance + Fantasy.

Some of these books are straight up fantasy...others or urban fantasy – set in the
real world, but with magic.

### *Re-Imagined Fairy Tales*

The Poisoned Princess

### *Crescent Isle Witches*

(Writing as Avery Glass)

Witch in the City

New Witch in Town

Witch on the Run

THERE'S ALWAYS TWO SIDES TO A STORY

# TWELVE DAYS
# OF
# *Christmas*

## HER SIDE OF THE STORY
## BOOK ONE

# EMMA LEA

# Day One

*14th December (local time)*
*Sydney International Airport, Sydney*

Ho freaking ho.

Is there anything more depressing than standing in the middle of a stupidly crazy busy airport twelve days out from Christmas and being entirely alone? If there is, then I have not experienced it. It's just my luck that my holiday season has been screwed to all hell because of one arsehole ex and one arsehole boss. It's not enough that my boyfriend of nearly eight months decided that the night before our tropical getaway was the best night to dump me, but then my boss thought it would be a fabulous idea to send me to freaking Siberia to try to get an interview with a reclusive and completely insane toy-shop tycoon. Okay, so New York is not exactly Siberia, but it may as well be.

I had my Christmas holidays sorted. Fourteen fabulous days of sun, sand, surf and sex. I thought for sure Michael was going to pop THE question in paradise. He'd been both very secretive and overly attentive to me. I'd even discovered a receipt from a jewellery store in his pants' pocket. I took a trip to the lingerie store to buy him a very special present as a reward. Instead, I got the 'it isn't you, it's me' speech with a 'I hope we can still be friends' thrown in for good luck.

Stupid freaking arsehole. I hope his man-parts shrivel up and fall off.

So, instead of my dream holiday on a remote island in the tropics, I'm going to New York where it's cold and miserable.

Like my heart.

*I'm dreaming of a white Christmas...*

Stupid bloody Christmas carols. There is no way I am dreaming of a white Christmas. I hate snow. I hate the cold. I hate Christmas. Bah humbug and all that jazz. I hate that even though I live in Australia, where Christmas is in the summer, I have to listen to Christmas songs extolling the virtues of snow and snowmen and sleigh rides and mistletoe. Mistletoe is a goddamn weed, a parasite that sucks the life out of any tree it clings to. Like Michael.

Taking a deep breath, I close my eyes to extinguish the rage consuming me. I need to find my zen. I have a twenty-plus hour flight in front of me, and it won't go well if I don't get a grip on my emotions. Thankfully, my boss sprang for business class tickets, and there will be alcohol. A small consolation for giving up my holiday in Bora Bora.

I open my eyes and turn, running smack dab into a very hard, warm, male chest. I look up into a pair of sparkling blue eyes above a wide smile, white teeth gleaming like a toothpaste commercial, and I scowl.

'Watch it,' I say, grabbing my bag and attempting to drag it towards the counter.

The stupid thing falls on its side and my carry on case, which was sitting on top of it, falls to the ground, popping open and spewing its contents all over the airport tiles. That includes the spare pair of panties I'd packed that just happen to be bright pink with white polka dots. Could this day get any worse?

'Here, let me help you with that,' a very male voice says.

I feel the flush of embarrassment followed closely by anger.

'I think you've done enough,' I reply as I scramble to get all my things packed back into the carry-on. I stand up and straighten my shirt. I'm not dressed to impress; I'm dressed for comfort. Twenty hours is a long bloody time to be on an airplane, so I choose to be comfortable. Stretchy yoga pants and an oversize t-shirt that has a tendency to slip off my shoulder. My mouse-brown and completely unruly curly hair is caught up in a messy bun, and sunglasses are on my face. I may have had a rather long date with a very good bottle of red last night. Sunglasses are required to protect my eyes from the self-righteous glare of the summer sun.

I turn to face my attacker, because it really is all his fault that this happened, and see the offending pair of pink knickers dangling from his index finger.

'Did you forget something?' he asks with a smirk.

I reach to grab them and he lifts them out of my reach.

'What do you say?'

'Give me back my underwear, you jerk!'

His smile widens despite my nastiness.

'What's the magic word?'

'Give me back my underwear you jerk, please?'

He laughs and hands them over to me. I do not like his laugh, not one bit. I don't like the way it makes me feel all warm on the inside and causes a shiver to run down my back. No, that is not attraction. That is repulsion. That wasn't a spectacular laugh; that was a creepy laugh. I stuff my panties into my bag and grab the handle of my suitcase once again, taking a deep breath and squaring my shoulders. Let's try an exit with dignity this time.

'Thanks,' I mumble as I walk away. I don't know why I thanked him, but the manners my mother drilled into me seem to come out at the most bizarre times.

The line for checking in snakes around the stretchy barriers five or six times, and I take my place at the end, even more out of sorts than I was when I entered the airport. My phone rings, and I dig it out of my handbag. When I see who's calling, I debate whether to answer, but self-preservation wins out.

'Hey Boss,' I say, feigning happiness.

'Isobel, I'm glad I caught you before you boarded.'

Maryanne is my boss, and most of the time I love her, but today she is on my shit list. Not that I would ever tell her that, because, well, she signs my pay checks. Actually, I probably would and probably have told her that a time or two, but I don't want to get into a fight with her today.

'What can I do for you Maryanne? I'm in line for check-in.'

'I just wanted to make sure you had all the details—'

I snort a laugh. 'Details? What details? The guy is a ghost. Nobody knows who he is or where he lives. Nobody can even give a definitive description of what he looks like. What makes you think I can?'

'You're my best investigative reporter,' she says. 'If anyone can do it, you can.'

'Stop blowing smoke up my arse. I was the only one available.'

'True, but you are my best. You won an award for the piece you did on the Prime Minister—'

'Look, I get it. You need me. What I don't get is why you need this story. Who cares about a super-secret Santa wannabe? It's not like he's curing cancer or negotiating world peace. This is a puff piece, and I don't do puff pieces.'

'This is more than a puff piece,' Maryanne says. 'There's a story here. This guy gives away millions of dollars in toys every year to kids all over the world. The opening of his very first toy shop is big news. There are rumours he's Australian.'

I blow out a breath as the line moves forward. 'Fine. I'll do my best, but I'm not promising anything.'

'I need that story by midnight Christmas Eve.' She hesitates before speaking again and something in her voice gives me pause. 'The magazine needs this story, Isobel. Don't let me down.'

'WHAT DO you mean I was downgraded to economy?' I screech at the woman behind the check-in counter.

'You haven't been downgraded,' she says reasonably, 'You were never booked into Business Class.'

'I don't bloody believe this,' I say, thumping my hand on the counter. 'There is no way I am flying sixteen thousand kilometres in economy. Now get me a bloody seat in Business Class or point me in the direction of someone who can.'

The people around me must think that I'm a real bitch. Today, yes, but normally? No, I'm sweet and kind and polite...okay, well maybe not sweet and kind, but I am usually polite and well mannered. I am stubborn and determined, and I can be ruthless in my job, but I'm still a nice person. This is me on a bad day. I'm entitled to a bad day, right?

'Is there a problem?' a familiar voice from behind me asks.

God, it's him. I can feel the warmth of his body through the back of my shirt as he stands close behind me. Too close.

'It's fine,' I say through gritted teeth. 'The airline just screwed up my booking and is now refusing to give me the seat I booked.'

'I'm sorry, ma'am, there are no more seats in Business Class. I have the seat you booked in economy or I have one First-Class seat left. It is Christmas, you know.'

'How much is the First-Class ticket?'

'Nine thousand dollars.'

'What the actual f—?' I stop myself just in time. I made a deal with my mother to tone down my swearing, today is testing my patience. I take a breath. 'That is twice the price of a Business Class seat and eight times the price of economy. Is the ticket dipped in gold? Do I get a full body massage and a magic pill to ensure I don't get jet lag?'

The woman looks at me like I am an escaped psych patient. 'The seats recline into beds, gourmet meals and a wide range of beverages are provided—'

'Forget it. I'll take the economy one. There is nothing you can offer me that will make me agree to pay such an exorbitant fee. Not even if Chris Hemsworth was giving me a full body massage and Chris Pine was feeding me grapes would I pay that much for a flight...okay, maybe, *maybe*, if the two Chris' were included, I'd consider it, but seeing as though they are not, economy it is.'

I hand over my passport and my ticket, lift my suitcase onto the conveyer belt.

'There will be a sixty-dollar fee for your luggage.'

'What!?'

'Your luggage is over the permitted weight—'

'Surely you can overlook that this time. It's not over by much and there has already been a mix up with her ticket...'

I look behind me to see him giving his charming smile to the woman behind the counter, his sparkling eyes flirting with her. There's even that movie star twinkle shining from the corner of his mouth as he shows her his gleaming white teeth. She flutters her lashes at him and her cheeks turn rosy. I roll my eyes.

'Don't worry—'

'Of course, sir,' she says with a smile and an indecent invitation in her eyes, 'We can waive the fee this time.' She turns to me and scowls, handing over my boarding pass. 'Gate Twenty-Three.'

I grab my boarding pass, bare my teeth at her in more of a warning than a smile, and turn from the counter, once again bumping into Prince Charming.

'You didn't need to do that,' I say as I manoeuvre around him, heading for the security gates and onto customs.

'It was my pleasure,' he says, calling after me.

I lift one hand in a wave without looking back. Thank God he isn't following me. How is it he has been witness to the two most embarrassing moments of my day? I sneak a look over my shoulder to make sure he really is gone, and I'm disappointed to find that he is nowhere to be found. Disappointed? Why should I feel disappointed? The guy is annoying; completely and utterly annoying. I'm glad he's gone, glad that I won't be seeing his smug smile or twinkly eyes again.

*We wish you a merry Christmas...*

'Oh, shut the hell up,' I mutter as I pass a group of carollers dressed in Victorian-era gowns. It's forty degrees in the shade outside the airport, so why the hell would they be wearing fur-lined bonnets and hand muffs like they are in some freaking pilgrim Christmas special? This is goddamn bloody Australia! We do Christmas in summer! Where are the hot guys in tiny Speedos? Where are the tanned and toned surfer dudes with their long sun-bleached blonde locks and their killer smiles? Why aren't those guys standing around wishing everyone a Merry Christmas and handing out Magnum Ice-creams or, better yet, Frozen Eggnog inspired daiquiris? Now, that I could get on board with.

I climb onto a barstool and order a cocktail. I've got a long flight ahead of me, smooshed into the back of the plane like cattle with fifty thousand other plebs. I need alcohol, STAT.

'Isobel Carmichael, please report to the information desk. Isobel Carmichael, please report to the information desk.'

Seriously? I haven't even gotten my drink yet and there is another crisis. I motion the bartender over.

'They're calling my name,' I say pointing up to the ceiling to indicate the voice over the PA system. 'Hold my spot?'

He winks and smiles at me. 'Sure thing, honey. Your drink will be waiting for you when you get back.'

I leave my carry-on bag on my seat, but take my handbag, and walk over to the information desk.

'I'm Isobel Carmichael,' I say, 'You were paging me?'

'Oh, yes, Ms Carmichael. The airline would like to apologise for the earlier mixup and upgrade you to First Class.'

'Are you serious?' I ask, not quite believing my luck. So far today— hell, this month—things haven't exactly gone my way.

'We are.' She hands me a new boarding pass, and I look down at the black inked 'First Class' like I am Charlie and have just found the last golden ticket for Wonka's Chocolate Factory.

'Thank you,' I say, gracing her with my first genuine smile of the day.

'Merry Christmas,' she replies and this time it doesn't make me scowl.

I wander back over to the bar where both my drink and my carry-on are waiting for me. The day is looking up.

UN-FREAKING BELIEVABLE. Please, don't let the seat next to him be my seat.

'Welcome to Qantas. Let me show you to your seat.'

I follow the flight attendant down the aisle, praying that I am not seated next to him, but nobody listens to my prayers.

'Here you go. Let me stow that luggage for you.'

I hand my carry-on to her and give her a once over. She is gorgeous, blonde hair swept up in a tidy french twist, not a hair out of place. Flawless makeup and a killer body. Tall, taller than me, skinnier than me, better looking than me. I sigh. I look like a slob compared to the beauty queen beside me. I shoot a quick glance to Prince Charming, expecting him to be making eyes at the flight attendant, except his eyes are on me.

'Would you like a glass of Champagne?' the fight attendant asks.

'God, yes,' I reply, falling into the plush leather seat.

'Hello again.'

I turn and give him a smile. It wouldn't hurt to be nice to him until we are in the air, then I intend to put in my headphones and escape into a stupid rom-com before falling into a blissful sleep.

'So you like Chris'?

'What?' I ask turning to him again.

'You like the name Chris...Chris Hemsworth, Chris Pine...'

'Oh, sorry, I thought you said Christmas. Yeah, I don't mind the name Chris, but it's more about the man...wait, is your name Chris?'

He smiles at me, a big, wide, cheerful smile. 'It's Christian, actually.'

'Do your friends call you Chris?'

He shakes his head, 'My mother would have a heart attack if people started calling me Chris. She has very strong opinions on nicknames.'

'Strong opinions as in she doesn't like them?'

'It is her opinion that if she had wanted me to be called Chris, she would have had that written on the birth certificate.'

'And what do you think?'

He shrugged, 'It doesn't bother me either way. What's in a name really...'

'You're not going to quote Shakespeare to me are you?'

'A rose by any other name—'

I roll my eyes and he laughs. 'Okay, no Shakespeare. But now I am at a disadvantage.'

'How so?'

'You know my name, but I am yet to know yours.'

'I'm Isobel. Isobel Carmichael.'

'Please to meet you Isobel Carmichael, I'm Christian Palmer.'

We shake hands, and I look him over. He looks familiar, but he couldn't be, could he?

'Ah. I know that look.'

'What look?' I ask innocently.

'The 'where do I know him from' look.'

'It's more of a 'he looks familiar' look.' I laugh.

He rolls his eyes, but doesn't seem to be annoyed. 'The answer is yes.'

'What was the question?'

'The 'are you related to' question that usually follows the look.'

'Ah,' I say knowingly. 'But I haven't quite worked out why I should know you. So are you going to tell me?'

'No,' he says with a grin. 'It will give you something to think about on this flight.'

The flight attendant returns with my Champagne, and the plane pulls away from the gate. I notice Christian's knuckles have turned white as he grips the armrests of his seat.

'First time flyer?' I ask with a sip of very delicious bubbly.

'No, I fly all the time,' he says, lightly, but there is tension around his eyes and his smile seems a little forced.

'Nervous flyer then?'

'Not exactly. I don't mind the flying bit, it's the taking off and landing that I'm not all that thrilled about.'

'You know that, statistically speaking, you are safer in a plane than in a car, right?'

'I don't really believe that statistic. I think a marketing company for an airline made it up. Regardless, if I am in a car and have a minor accident, I am likely to walk away from it. The same can not be said of a minor accident while on a jumbo jet.'

By this time the plane is taxiing to the runway and the flight attendants are doing their safety demonstrations.

'Look,' I say, pointing to the choreographed presentation. 'You get a life jacket with a whistle and a light. We'll be fine.'

'Those will not help when we crash in a fiery explosion at the end of the runway.'

'True,' I say conversationally.

'They will also be useless if we are falling from thirty thousand feet. A life jacket is not a parachute.'

I shrug. 'We're probably more likely to die in a fiery explosion than die from falling out of the plane.'

9

'Not helping,' he says as the plane lines up and speeds down the runway.

'So once we're in the air, you're fine?'

'Generally,' he says through clenched teeth.

'Lightening or bird strikes don't concern you?'

'Are you trying to give me a panic attack?'

I laugh as the plane lifts off and there is that tiny moment of weight-lessness. I love flying, and taking off is my favourite part of the entire experience.

'We survived!'

He scowls at me and I just laugh, draining the last of my champagne as the plane climbs into the sky.

'So Christmas,' he says, straightening in his seat and running a hand through his hair.

'What about it?'

'Well, you snapped at me when you thought I asked if you like Christmas. There has to be a story there.'

I shrug, looking around for a flight attendant to supply me with another glass of wine. 'I'm not a fan of the most commercialised holiday of the year.'

His eyebrows rise. 'You don't like Christmas? Everyone loves Christmas.'

'Yeah, well, not me.'

'Not even when you were a kid? Who stole your Christmas joy?'

'You're not going to stop badgering me until I tell you, are you?'

'It's a long flight, and I'm interested in why someone as young and pretty as you is so cynical about the happiest time of the year.'

'Oh God, you sound like a commercial or a Christmas special.'

He laughs good-naturedly. 'I admit, I do love Christmas. There is something magical about it. It makes you believe in miracles.'

Is this guy for real?

'Christmas has never been special or magical to me. We didn't cele-brate it when I was growing up.'

'For religious reasons?'

'No, not particularly... well, I suppose in a way. My family is agnos-tic, if that is even the right word, and my mother was more about celebrating the Summer Solstice by burning my favourite toys in sacrifice to the great Goddess in the sky.'

'What? Are you serious?'

Unfortunately, I am serious.

I nod. 'Yep. My mother cobbled together different beliefs from a range of religions. She believes we find true religion within us, so whatever ritual or tenet that resonates with you is your truth, your religion.'

'And how does that fit in with burning your toys?'

I sigh. 'She believes that by sacrificing our most prized possession, we will be blessed tenfold.'

'That's crazy,' he says with a shake of his head. 'So instead of receiving gifts at Christmas, you had to give up your favourite thing. That's just cruel.'

I shrug. 'I didn't really understand until I started school and the kids were writing letters to Santa and asking for things. When I asked my mother about it, she lectured me on the evils of consumerism and materialistic thinking.'

'How old were you?'

'Five.'

'So what did you do on Christmas Day?'

'Dished out food at a local soup kitchen.'

'Oh well, I suppose that's in the spirit of Christmas. So you've never gotten a Christmas gift or had the joy of opening a Christmas stocking on Christmas morning?'

I shake my head.

'And you've never left carrots and beer out for Santa and his reindeer on Christmas Eve or looked into the sky and wondered if the stars were his sleigh?'

I shake my head again. 'Nope.'

'That's just sad.'

'I got gifts as I got older, from friends and work colleagues.' I look at him and am surprised to see pity in his eyes. 'Hey, don't sweat it. You can't miss what you've never had.'

'You don't miss it?'

I shook my head. 'I really don't. There's so much pressure to buy the right gift and to spend all that money on something that will be forgotten before the week is out.'

'But Christmas is more than just material things. It's about family and giving and love and forgiveness.'

'Every day should be about those things. I don't see why we need a special day for that.'

He sits back in his seat and studies me. 'You are a fascinating person Isobel Carmichael.'

Why does that make me tingle all over?

# Day Two

*14<sup>th</sup> December (local time)*
*JFK International Airport, New York*

I have just flown nearly six thousand kilometres in over twenty-one hours, and it's still the same goddamn day that I left. It's five thirty in the afternoon, and it's dark and cold and snowing, and my luggage is lost. I waited by the carousel watching every single person on my flight retrieve their luggage, but mine didn't come through the magic door.

I'm now waiting in front of the service counter while they search their computers to try to find where my bag might have ended up.

'Bora Bora,' the man says, giving me a sympathetic stare. 'Your luggage is in Bora Bora.'

'Well, that's just freaking fabulous. My luggage gets the vacation I gave up for my boss. Excellent.'

'We can have it here by tomorrow afternoon. The next day at the latest.'

'And what am I meant to do in the meantime?' I look down at the short black skirt I'm wearing. Thankfully, as well as my pink panties, I also had a change of clothes in my carry-on. I might have wanted to travel in comfort, but I had no intention of walking through the New York airport in my yoga pants. My skirt, calf-length boots, crisp white wrap shirt and black wool swing coat look great, but I have no desire to wear them for the next three days.

'There's not much more we can do, I'm afraid.' He looks sorry, but in my head I can hear him saying 'sorry, not sorry' and I want to punch him.

'Fine,' I say through gritted teeth, 'I'm staying at Park Place.' I've always wanted to say that. Such an iconic hotel that has featured in so many movies, and I am actually going to be staying there. Maryanne is really trying to sweeten this deal; she must really want this story.

'Certainly, Ms Carmichael. Can I get you a cab?'

I shake my head. 'No, thank you,' I say and walk away. That's another New York dream, hailing an infamous yellow cab.

I walk towards the exit, feeling a little Carrie Bradshaw-ish as I step outside and into New York City.

Bloody hell, it's cold. I am definitely not wearing enough layers, and the cold December wind cuts right through me. My skirt barely reaches my knees, and my boots only go halfway up my calves. I don't have any stockings or tights on, and the expanse of flesh between boots and skirt is now turning blue. My beautiful summer tan is reduced to goose-bumps, and a tremor goes through me as another gust of wind steals my breath. I could be in Bora Bora right now... with my luggage.

If I don't get a cab now, I'll freeze to death. Stepping closer to the busy road, I don't notice the precariousness of the wet, icy pavement before it bucks me off. I end up on my arse, flashing bystanders with my pink polka-dot undies. That hurt, and it's freezing cold and wet, and now my skirt is soaked through. To say nothing of my panties. And to top it off, someone trips over me and spills hot coffee all over me. Now my skirt is ruined, my shirt is ruined, my arse hurts and I officially hate New York.

A pair of strong, warm arms lift me from my puddle of misery, and I turn into the hard chest as his arms encircle me.

'It's okay. I've got you.'

Why? Why is he always there when I make a fool of myself? I think the universe hates me.

'Christian?' I say looking up into his sparkling blue eyes. 'What are you doing here?'

'I saw you waiting for a cab and thought I'd offer you a ride.'

I swallow down the lump in my throat and will the tears in my eyes not to fall. I'm just tired and wet and cold and hurt. It's not because he is being nice to me when I've been nothing but a bitch to him.

'Where's you luggage?'

'Bora Bora,' I squeak past the sob stuck to my vocal chords.

'They lost your luggage?' He looks down at me with such concern that a single tear slips down my cheek as I nod. 'Oh, honey,' he says, wiping the tear away with a gloved thumb. 'Come on, let me give you a ride. Where are you staying?'

'Park Place,' I manage to get out.

'Okay, let's go.'

He leads me towards a black limousine, and a chauffeur opens the door for me. I slide across the buttery soft leather and stare at Christian. Who the hell is this guy? Christian Palmer. His name is so familiar, but it's just out of reach of my tired brain. He slides in beside me, and the door closes. I'm too overwrought to speak as I take in the car and the man. He really is good-looking, something that I had taken little notice of until now.

'You never told me who you are.' I say.

He turns and grins at me. 'Of course I did. I'm Christian Palmer.'

'Okay, Christian Palmer, what is it that you do?'

'If I told you that, it would be cheating,' he says.

I squint at him, trying to work out where I have seen his face before. It's a gorgeous face, square-shaped with a firm jaw and just enough scruff to be sexy and not untidy. His nose is slightly crooked, like it may have been broken in the past, and his lips are kissable. Wait, what? I didn't mean that. I don't want to kiss him. Lifting my eyes from his lips, I notice he is watching me, and I was staring at his lips for way too long. I lick my own suddenly dry lips, and his eyes drop to them, darkening. Whew, it's suddenly hot in here.

The limousine comes to a stop, and the door is opened. Christian's eyes linger on me for a moment longer before he slides out of the car and turns back to offer me his hand.

'Welcome to Park Place,' the door man says as we enter the lobby.

I am way underdressed not to mention a mess from my tumble on the sidewalk and I feel decidedly out of place in this plush room. Christian prompts me with a hand on the small of my back and we walk to the reception desk. The front desk woman takes one look at me and her face clouds over. I must look worse than I thought. Her eyes glance to the side and she sees Christian and her face transforms.

'Mr Palmer, lovely to see you again. Are you checking in?'

'No,' he says with a smile. 'Not this time, but my friend is.'

The woman looks at me again and scowls. 'Name?'

'Isobel Carmichael,' I say with as much snobbery as I can mange. 'Or it may be under Iconoclast.'

'The magazine?' Christian asks with a raised eyebrow.

I nod. 'I write for the magazine.'

'Here is your key Ms Carmichael,' the front desk woman says handing me a keycard.

'Looks like you're all checked in,' Christian says, his hands in his pockets as he looks around the lobby.

'Thank you,' I say, feeling uncharacteristically shy. 'For the lift and for rescuing me.'

He turns his superstar smile on me and for the first time I see what every other woman has been drooling over for the last twenty-four hours.

'I'm glad I met you Isobel Carmichael,' he says and then turns and walks away.

With a sigh, I turn to the bank of elevators, thoughts of food and bed crowding out the moment of attraction I feel towards a man I will probably never see again.

My room is on the second floor, and it's quite a trek from the elevators to get to it. I finally reach the door and stick my card in the slot, but the damned thing doesn't open. I jiggle the handle and try again. The light stays red. I take a deep breath and slowly insert the card again, and the light turns green. I breathe a sigh of relief and push the door open.

The room is dark and stuffy, almost too warm after the frigid temperature outside. I slip the card into the slot by the door, and the lights come on, revealing a long corridor. I drag my bag down the hall and come into the room proper. It's a single room with a double bed sitting in the centre of the side wall. There is barely enough space to manoeuvre around the bed. I put my bag on the luggage stand and take in my surroundings. This is not the room I have seen in the movies.

A drab brown comforter that has seen better days covers the bed. The carpet is worn and patchy in places, and the dark drapes are heavy and dusty. All in all, it has the feel of a cheap motel. I should have stayed at The Mayfield; at least they know me there, and I would've gotten a decent room.

Maybe I at least have a view of Central Park. I walk over to the drapes and whip them open with a dramatic flourish. What I thought was a floor to ceiling window is a pokey little porthole. They used over-sized drapes to camouflage the tiny window. It's too dark to see the view, but I can't see the lights of the city, so I expect I will be looking directly at another building come morning. I pull the drapes shut in disgust.

What a disappointment New York has turned out to be. I can't even go out and explore the city because I have no clothes to change into. I pick up the room service menu and place a call to the kitchen. If I can't go out, at least I can eat some authentic New York food and flick through the abundance of television channels. I am looking forward to seeing the mythical thousands of channels available to Americans.

I strip out of my wet clothes and give them a bit of a wash in the bath, hanging them over the towel rail to dry so I can wear them tomorrow. Back in my comfy—if a little gross—yoga pants and t-shirt, I make myself comfortable on the bed and switch on the television. A knock on the door heralds my dinner, and I gladly tip the room service guy and settle back on the bed with my authentic American hamburger and fries.

Finally, something is going my way. I find a crime show to watch and happily stuff my face. I kick off the blanket as I warm up and reach for my water. By the time the show is finished, I'm sweating. I look around trying to find the air controls and scramble off the bed to adjust them. It's a dial-looking thing, and I move it just a notch and then crawl back onto the bed, flicking through the channels before settling on a movie.

My eyes are drooping and the jet lag is catching up with me, but I fight it, wanting to at least stay awake until nine to combat the jet lag, but it's a struggle. The movie isn't holding my attention, and my thoughts keep drifting to Christian. I should Google him, but that would be cheating, wouldn't it? I'm usually good with faces and names; it's important in my job to recall the details so I can beef up my article with the nuances of an interview, not just the words. But I am at a loss as to remember how I know Christian. He's obviously someone of note; the lady at the front desk recognised him. The first-class airline ticket and the long limousine that picked him up tell me he's wealthy. I assume he's Australian, although he has one of those accents that make it hard to determine his country of origin, so he probably doesn't spend a lot of time back home.

I really like the way his eyes sparkle. It's like looking at the ocean on a summer day with the bright sun glinting off the waves. And when he smiles, it warms me all over. When he held me close and wrapped his arms around me, it felt like being wrapped up in a comfy blanket. He is a big man, with broad shoulders and a firm chest. I could feel the definition of his muscles through his dress shirt as he pulled me close. The guy has it all going on under his clothes.

Which is a dangerous road for my mind to go down. I have no right to imagine Christian without clothes on, but it's like trying not to think of an elephant; I can't help but think of an elephant. The more I try not to imagine just what he is hiding under his suit and topcoat, the more vivid the picture becomes. I'm a terrible person. I've only just broken up with my long-term boyfriend, and I'm already fantasising about another man... a man I met less than twenty-four hours ago. But I can't help it; I'm weak-willed and horny. There was definitely a spark of something between us, and I know that if we ever got up close and personal, we would burn up the sheets. But that's not happening... it can't happen... I won't be seeing him again.

Sleep finally claims me, and Christian—a very naked Christian—is the last thing I think about as I drop off into sleep.

MY FIRST CONSCIOUS thought is that I am freezing, like literally freezing. I'm sure my lips are blue, and I'm only minutes away from hypothermia. I crack open my eye, taking a moment to determine where I am, and then I roll over and look at the bedside clock. It's only ten o'clock at night. I've only been asleep for two hours at the most, and now I'm wide awake.

The sheets and comforter are wrapped around me to ward off the chill, but I'm still freezing. I roll off the bed, staying wrapped in my cocoon, and shuffle-jump my way across the room to the air-conditioning control. Somehow, the tiny bit I moved it took it from Sahara to Antarctic. It seems that the air conditioner only has those two settings. I hate the cold, so I move the dial back to its original spot. At least I can strip off until I'm wearing nothing and pretend I'm in the tropics if it gets too hot. I'd prefer that to turning into a block of ice.

I turn around to make my way back to the bed, but the comforter gets caught under my foot and I take a tumble. My arms are wrapped up in the cocoon, so I have no way of stopping myself from hitting the floor. I knock my head on the corner of the bed on the way down and see stars. I lie on the floor where I landed and wonder what deity I pissed off. It is the only explanation for the run of bad luck I've had over the last week, starting with the abandonment of my boyfriend and ending with me lying on the floor of a hotel with a possible concussion.

Not ready to get up just yet, I stare at the ceiling. I'm entitled to a little pity party, and now seems like the perfect time for it to happen. Sniffling, the tears leak from my eyes to run down the side of my head and into my ears. I'm a hot mess in my airplane-smelling clothes and the ridiculously inadequate comforter, which, by the way, is not comforting at all.

What am I doing here? What did I do wrong? The next two weeks were meant to be all about fun. I'm still young and vibrant and exciting, so why the hell am I lying here all alone in a city I hate in the middle of bloody winter when all my dreams take place in the sun and surf?

There's a loud 'pop-pop-pop' outside my window and a few shouted curses before a car drives off. Great, a gang shooting outside my window—the perfect thing to top off the perfect freaking day. I hear the sirens next, and I roll to my side, wishing I could transport myself home with teleportation. The last thing I want to do is get back on another plane for twenty hours. Not to mention I'm here for a job, a job I don't want and have no clue how to even start. This 'Mr Toys' guy sounds like a crackpot to me. A Santa try-hard with too many dollars and not enough sense.

I gradually get to my feet and climb back on the bed, snuggling into the pillow and closing my eyes, trying to go back to sleep. For the first time, I realise how noisy the streets are. I can hear every car, every siren. I swear I can even hear the pedestrians on the street as they yap their way past the hotel. How am I supposed to sleep with all this racket going on?

I fight my way out of the bedding-burrito I made and reach for the TV controls. I switch it on and search the channels for some music. At least I can drown out the sound of the street with some decent tunes. I snuggle back into my nest and close my eyes, but now my brain is awake, and I'm once again thinking about Christian. The guy is just as annoying in my imagination as he is in real life. Every time I turned around yesterday, there he was, and now he is invading my thoughts. What is it about him that he can't leave me alone?

I need a distraction. I need ice-cream. I pick up the room service menu again and discover they have a tasting plate of seven different Ben & Jerry's ice cream flavours. Perfect, that's exactly what I need. At least if I'm stuffing my face with ice-cream, I won't be thinking of him. I pick up the phone and order the ice-cream, adding a brownie just for the heck of it.

Dragging my handbag over to me, I search through it for my iPad and hit the Apple Books icon. I stuffed it full of books before I left home, and now is the perfect time to delve into my dirty little secret. I may write very serious and hard-hitting news articles, but I like to read romance. Hot, sexy, dirty, sweet, romance—I love them all. I'm a sucker for a happy ending.

There is a knock at the door and I scramble out of my blankets to answer the door. The room service guy hands me the tray of dessert and I thank him with a big tip. There is a hell of a lot of ice-cream on this tray, but I don't care. I can't even remember the last time I indulged in my favourite treat. But if there was ever a time to indulge, it is right now. My day couldn't have been worse and at least this will go a little way towards making me feel better.

Settled back in my nest, I dig in while reading about a little bit of BDSM at the hands of a hot, sexy bad boy. Perfect.

# Day Three

T he sun beats down on me, and I relish the warmth of its rays. I can hear the surf breaking on the shore. The sand is soft beneath me, and only two things would make this even more perfect than it already is: a hot man and a cold drink.

I turn my head. *'Hey babe, can you get me one of those pretty coloured fruity cocktails with the umbrella in them?'*

*'No worries, babe,'* Christian says, smiling at me as his blue eyes sparkle.

I sit up, breaking free of the dream. I'm not in Bora Bora, I'm not laying in the sun working on my tan. I'm not with Christian.

I look around the dark room, getting my bearings. I'm in New York bloody City in the middle of winter in a hotel room that has seen better days. It may be the middle of winter outside, but because of the faulty heating in the room, it has to be close to forty degrees centigrade in here and I have stripped down to just my panties in the middle of the night to get some relief from the heat. But it isn't just the air-conditioning that is making me hot.

I'd been dreaming about Christian.

Okay, that has to stop, and it has to stop now. There is no way I am ever going to see that guy again, and dreaming about him half-naked will not do me any good. I take a sip of the water on my bedside and lay back down. It really is hot, even a little too hot, and for me that is saying something. But I can't risk adjusting the temperature again, so I'll just lay here and sweat it out—so much better than the alternative.

I let my eyes drift shut. The drone of the traffic outside my window is almost hypnotic and if I try really hard, I can almost imagine that it is the sound of waves breaking. The reggae music playing softly on the television helps my fantasy. I will the sound to lull me back to sleep and I drift in that lazy place between actual sleep and actual awake. The heat of the room, the drone of the traffic/waves, the music, and I can transport myself to my dream holiday spot. A deserted beach of pure white sand and crystal clear, turquoise water with the warm sun beating down.

An almighty crash and the tinkling of broken glass jolts me awake. The roar of a beast and the grinding of machinery followed by the irritating beeping noise of a truck when it is backing up. What in the ever loving hell is going on?

I jump out of bed and creep over to the window, parting the drapes just enough so I can see out. An orange strobe light catches my attention, lighting the area outside my room. Finally I glimpse the view I will be treated to when the sun finally rises. An alley. A bloody alley complete with stinky dumpsters and garbage trucks. I part the drapes further and lean against the cool glass to get a better look. It's so horrible that I can't look away and the cold glass feels good on my over-heated skin. No park view for me, no, that would be too much. I get the back alley, the place where they dump all the trash. And isn't that just a metaphor for my life?

One of the garbologists looks up and a toothy grin splits his face. What the hell is he smiling at? He raises his hand and gives me the thumbs up which is when I realise that I'm not wearing a shirt and I have my naked breasts pressed up against the glass. I'm flashing the goddamned garbo. Great. That's just bloody great.

I jump away from the glass and slam the drapes closed. Dammit! I'm going to do some serious damage to this hotel's TripAdvisor page. Park Place is supposed to be a hotel that has no bad rooms. One of those mythical places where every room is big and beautiful and has a view, whether of the city skyline or the infamous Central Park. In reality, I'm in the smallest, least impressive room with busted air conditioning and a view of the dumpsters.

This entire trip is doomed. Nothing has gone right from the moment I stepped through the doors of the airport in Sydney. Only I could end up in a situation where a man I have never met before dangles my panties from his finger in the middle of the airport concourse. Maybe there was something to my mother's cooky belief that the universe needs a sacrifice in order to bestow blessings. It had been a while since I'd partaken of her particular brand of crazy, and my life had been getting noticeably worse.

God, I must be in a bad state if I'm putting any stock in my mother's twisted beliefs. Maybe it was all those chain letters I ignored as a kid or those Facebook posts I didn't share despite the dire warning attached to them. Whatever it is, there is some serious bad juju hanging around me, and I have no idea how I'm going to shake it off. This did not bode well for finding the mysterious Mr Toys and convincing him to do an interview with me.

There is another loud crash as the garbage truck outside my window empties another dumpster. I look at the clock; it is 3:15 am. The witching hour. Perfect, just freaking perfect. As if my life needed anymore bad luck.

I pull a pillow over my head and will myself back to sleep. It's times like this I wish I believed in things like astro-travel, then I could will myself to Bora Bora and leave this pathetic phase of my life for some fun in the sun, even if it is for just a night. Anything would be better than staying here in this miserable room.

THE NEXT TIME I open my eyes, it's daylight. Thank God. I stare at the ceiling for a moment and wonder what woke me from my dreamless sleep. There's a knock at my door, and I sit up. That's what it was.

'Just a minute,' I call, rolling off the bed and looking for some clothes.

I drag the well-worn t-shirt over my head and pull up my yoga pants, hopping to the door as one foot gets stuck. I finger-comb my unruly curls and hope to God I don't have sleep in my eyes or dried drool on my chin, and I open the door. The young guy on the other side of the door takes a step back and grimaces before schooling his features. Surely I don't look that bad, do I?

'Ms Carmichael?' he asks tentatively.

'Yes,' I reply with all the dignity I can muster.

He shoves a Christmas gift bag at me. 'This came for you.'

I take the bag, curious to know who would send me a gift. Maybe this is Maryanne's way of making up for the crappy room she booked me.

'Ah, thanks,' I say, looking around for my wallet.

I give him a tip and he turns to walk away before turning back to me.

'Do you want me to send up an ice pack for that?' he asks.

'What?' I say stupidly.

'Never mind,' he says and walks away.

What the hell is he talking about? I dump the gift bag on the bed and squeeze into the minuscule bathroom, turning on the light and looking in the mirror. I scream and then lean closer to the mirror for a better look. There is an egg the size of a cricket ball on the side of my head and a nice purple bruise across the top of my eyelid, puffing up my eye and making me look like the loser of a prize fight.

Is it too early in the day to start drinking?

I drag my feet as I walk out of the bathroom. Maybe I could just hole up in my room today? There's no need to go outside. It's cold and wet, and I don't have enough clothes. The hotel will bring me food, and I have my laptop and the television, so what more could I need?

The bright red gift bag brightens me for a moment. I wonder what Maryanne sent me. It better be good to make up for this shitty trip. If she wants a story by Christmas eve, then things had better start looking up for me.

I peek inside the bag which is stuffed with tissue paper. Not able to keep my curiosity in check any longer, I pull out the festive paper, tossing it on the floor to get to the gift inside. Directly under the tissue paper are a pair of long, red and white striped socks. Seriously? These things are long enough to reach the middle of my thighs. I toss them on the bed thinking that this is my boss' idea of a joke. The next thing I pull out is a super soft, but super ugly Christmas sweater. Are you kidding me? I've heard about American's and their obsession with ugly Christmas sweaters, the Australian equivalent is an ugly Christmas t-shirt, but there is no way I am wearing this.

At the bottom of the bag is an envelope. I tear it open to read the note inside...

*I thought you might be cold so here's something to keep you warm.*
*Christian*

Of course it's from him. No one else would send me such ridiculous items. I lift the sweater and take in all its ugly glory. It's red with a rein-deer on it, who is spewing Christmas decorations out of its mouth. Charming. Classy. Surely a guy like him could have sprung for some-thing nicer. He's not poor, if the first-class air travel and the limousine are any judge of the matter.

My phone rings, and I pick it up distractedly.

'Go for Isobel Carmichael,' I say.

'Isobel, how is New York?'

I roll my eyes. 'Maryanne,' I say in return.

'Is it gorgeous? How is the hotel?'

'The hotel is a dump. They gave me the absolute worst room in the place with the wonderfully exciting view of an alley complete with New York dumpsters. And what the hell was with you booking me an economy seat? You promised me business class!'

'Oh, well, that. You see—'

'Save it,' I say. 'It doesn't matter now. The room, however, is awful. The air conditioner only has two settings, Sahara or Antarctica, and the sheets and bedspread have seen better days. At least the bed is soft and the pillows are great—'

'Oh, well, there is that at least—'

'And the airline lost my luggage, so I'm stuck here with no clothes, not even a change of underwear, Maryanne! I don't know why I let you talk me into these things. I could be sitting on a beach in Bora Bora sipping a cocktail with my luggage, but no, I'm freezing my arse off in New York City in the middle of goddamned winter!'

Maryanne is silent on the other end of the phone. She is used to my tantrums, so I'm not concerned about yelling at her. We have that kind of relationship... I rant and rave, and she sits quietly by, letting me have my say, and then I end up doing whatever she wants, anyway. It's dysfunctional, but it works.

'Are you done?'

'Yeah,' I say with a sigh, flopping down on the bed.

'Okay, good. I have a tip for you. Mr Toys is rumoured to be attending a luncheon at your hotel today.'

'How on earth could you know that? Nobody even knows who he is. Where are you getting your information from?'

'I can't reveal my source,' she says cryptically. 'I just need you to crash that luncheon and see if you can scope him out.'

Damn. That means no hiding out in my room today. I check the time; it's just after ten. I should have time to slip out and find somewhere to buy some clothes before the luncheon starts.

'What time?'

'One o'clock,' Maryanne says. 'Good luck.'

She disconnects, and I lie there for a moment staring at the ceiling and wondering when my life got so out of control.

I MANAGE TO SHOWER, but the water pressure is crap and the stupid thing goes cold while I'm in the middle of washing my hair. Considering the temperature in my room, it isn't too bad, though. My white shirt is ruined with no hope of salvation. New York coffee stains like a bitch. With no other options and praying that people will just think I'm full of Christmas cheer, I don the striped socks and ugly-arse sweater with my black skirt and boots. Checking myself in the mirror, I don't look too bad, sort of like a rebel elf, except for the spewing reindeer on my sweater. I grab my coat and my handbag and step out of the room. The drop in temperature is a welcome relief. Why can't have the same balmy warmth in my room? I'll have to speak to the front desk otherwise I'm going to die of heat exhaustion.

I make the lengthy trek back to the elevators and head for the lobby. My dark glasses hide the black eye, and I pull my hair over the lump. Makeup covered some of the damage, but not enough to hide my clumsiness completely. I glide across the lobby floor towards the front desk and pretend that everyone is looking at me because they think I'm a famous movie star rather than because I look like a Christmas party reject. It's amazing what it does to your self-esteem when you have a vivid imagination like mine.

'Good morning ma'am,' the front desk man says, taking in my dark glasses and strange get-up without blinking an eye.

'Good morning,' I say sweetly. Yes, I can be sweet when I want to be. That old catch-more-flies-with-honey thing is one of the many tools I use in my journalist toolbox. 'I was just wondering if the airline has called about my luggage? They seemed to have sent it to Bora Bora instead of New York and they assured me it would be here today.'

There's a flash of relief in his eyes before he masks it with his professional gaze. He's glad that my attire is the result of misplaced luggage and not a crazy fashion statement. It wouldn't do to have someone with my taste and style schlepping through his high-class lobby disturbing his guests. This is the conversation I imagine is going on in his head, and it pisses me off. But I keep my cool. There will be no temper tantrums or frustrated crying from me today. Today is going to be better. Things are going to go my way from this moment on.

'I'm sorry, ma'am,' he says, looking at me with pity. 'There is nothing here from the airline.'

I clench my jaw and give him a tight smile. It's okay, I tell myself. The airline said this afternoon, and it's not afternoon yet. It could still arrive today and save me from having to wear this sweater again.

'Okay, well thank you. Um, by the way, is there any chance that someone could check the heating in my room?'

'What seems to be the problem?'

'It is ridiculously hot, and as much as I like tropical weather, last night was too hot even for me.'

'I'll have maintenance have a look at it.'

'Thank you,' I say, keeping it pleasant. I do not want to be branded as one of those complaining guests. I can be sweet when I want to be. 'Could you possibly point me toward the nearest clothing boutique?'

He waves over a bellboy. 'Please get Ms Carmichael a cab to Macy's.'

'Yes, sir,' the young guy says before turning to me with a smile. 'Right this way ma'am.'

Geez. I wish they would all stop calling me ma'am. It makes me feel like I'm a middle-aged matron not a young, hip twenty-something... okay, well a young, hip nearly thirty-something.

We step through the doors and into the frigid arctic weather, causing a shiver to run through me. How do these people live here? Winter for me barely dips below ten degrees, although Sydney has the odd frosty morning, nothing compared to this though. At least today I am dressed more appropriately, and despite the Christmas elf stockings, I'm glad I have them on to keep me warm.

The bellboy lifts his arm and a yellow cab screeches to a halt in front of us. He opens the door for me and leans in to give the driver instructions. I slide into the worn leather back seat and stare unabashedly at a sight I have only ever seen in movies. I may be a hard-hitting journalist, but this is my first ever trip to the U.S. It's kind of surreal to find yourself in a scene from a movie.

The cab takes off, joining the bumper to bumper traffic heading away from the park and towards another New York icon, Macy's Department Store. The trip is a blur, and before I know it, the cab has come to a stop. I dig in my purse for some money and hand it over before getting out and staring in amazement at the sight before me. Sydney high street does some pretty impressive Christmas window displays, but this one blows them out of the water. I walk into the store in a daze, overcome by everything Christmas.

❄

A COUPLE OF HOURS LATER, I emerge from the shopping mecca that is Macy's with bags hanging from every arm. Even if my luggage never arrives, I have bought enough stuff to get me through the rest of my stay. From underwear to stylish outfits, shoes and toiletries, I have it all and I am in shopper's heaven. No buyer's remorse for me even though my credit card is wheezing with exhaustion.

A cab takes me back to Park Place, the euphoria of the ultimate shopping experience still buzzing in my system. The luncheon I was supposed to be at is over, but I don't really care. I am on a shopping high. It's what I imagine runners get—not that I would know because I don't run—but I've heard rumours that such a thing exists.

The cab pulls up outside the hotel, and a doorman helps me and my shopping bags from the cab. I walk into the lobby feeling like a million bucks and run smack into a familiar chest. I pull my glasses down and look up into those twinkling blue eyes, stunned for a moment.

'We really need to stop meeting like this,' he says and then his brows creases in concern and his hand lifts to brush my hair away from my forehead. 'What happened?'

I feel my cheeks heat and clear my throat, taking a step back so that we are no longer touching from chest to knee.

'I fell and hit my head,' I say like it is the most natural thing in the world.

'Ouch,' he says, his mouth still pulled down. 'Does it hurt?'

Not until that moment it didn't. Now I'm reminded of the injury, and a headache pounds behind the egg on my head.

'It's not too bad.'

'It looks pretty bad.'

'Thanks,' I say grumpily. 'You sure know how to make a girl feel good.'

He laughs. 'Sorry.' His gaze sweeps over me from head to toe. 'I like the socks; they suit you. Sort of makes you look like a naughty Christmas elf.'

'Really? Was that your intention when you sent them to me?' I ask with a smirk.

He blushes and smiles sheepishly. 'Well, you did need something to keep those fantastic legs warm.'

I take a step forward and rest my hand on his chest. 'So, do naughty elves have to deal with those boys who make it onto Santa's naughty list?'

It's his turn to clear his throat and I watch with satisfaction as his eyes darken.

'Have you been a naughty boy, Christian?'

'Ah—'

'Mr Palmer!' His reply is interrupted by the concierge. 'Mr Palmer, do you have a moment?'

The moment breaks, and I step away, embarrassed by my flirting. I don't even like the guy, so what the hell am I thinking coming on to him like that? I pick up my bags and make my escape while he is distracted. If I don't get away from him now, there is no telling what could happen. Whenever he's around, I find myself doing and saying things that I would never normally do or say. He's bad for me, and I need to stay the hell away from him.

# Day Four

*16th December*
*Starbucks, New York City*

There had been no relief to the heat in my room overnight, but at least I was prepared this time. I'd even bought a pair of ear muffs to block out the noise of the street and the early wake-up call of the garbage truck in the alley. I may have been stuck in a sucky room, but I was determined not to let it beat me.

Dressed to impress in one of my new outfits, I am currently ensconced in a warm Starbucks, sipping a pumpkin-spiced latte and researching the enigma that is Mr Toys. There is both a lot written about him and not much said, if that makes any sense. Every year at this time, some plucky reporter does an exposé on the reclusive benefactor, but to date, no one has actually found him. There was speculation, rumours and conspiracy theories, but no one had ever come close to discovering his real identity.

My investigative juices are flowing. Maryanne is right; there is a story here. Why would a person donate so many toys over the years and not reveal who he is? Why the secrecy? Is he someone famous? Maybe he is a woman? There has never been any calling card saying specifically that he is a man. The media were the ones to christen him Mr Toys. Maybe who I am really looking for is a Mrs Toys.

He has to be old, I decide. There are stories dating back to the Second World War. Children in orphanages, displaced and orphaned by war, told of receiving anonymous gifts on Christmas morning. With each year that passed, more and more children received presents, always toys, never socks or shoes or anything practical. From what I can decipher, it all started in Australia and slowly spread across the world. Maybe there isn't just one person, but many. They may not even be connected. Which would be all well and good apart from the fact that there had been an ad run in every major newspaper in the world telling one and all that the mysterious Mr Toys is opening his very first toyshop in New York City. Tickets to the opening had been by ballot, and one hundred lucky nobodies had been picked to hobnob with the rich and famous at the Toyland Extravaganza to be held Christmas Eve eve. The store itself is to open on Christmas Eve, the morning after the Extravaganza.

It leaves me wondering why. Why after all this time is he making such a public declaration? What has changed to make him want to come out of the closet, as it were? It doesn't make sense. Everyone is expecting a big announcement at the Extravaganza. They're expecting to meet him, socialise with him, and finally find out who the hell he is. Maybe he is dying, and this is his last chance.

And that would be sad. As much as I don't like Christmas, what he does for the underprivileged children in the world is something to be admired. Food and clothing and a roof over their heads are basic human rights that every person deserves, but even with those things, kids also need a reminder that they are still kids, and the best way to do that is to give them a toy. Even if it is one day out of a long line of miserable ones, Mr Toys gives something magical to those children. I wouldn't be surprised to find out that he gives in other ways too. He probably gives large donations anonymously or through a dummy corporation, because no one could give a child a toy when they knew the child needed food. The toy is to encourage the children to believe in magic, to feed their souls, but I would bet every last dollar I have that he feeds their bodies too.

Which means he has to have a means of supporting his philanthropy. The man has to be made of money or have a way to continue making money to support his habit. Maybe that's why he is finally opening the store, to recoup some of the funds he gives away every year. It would be disappointing to find out that this venture is purely for money-making means, but I suppose the guy has to make his money somehow. The fact that all the toys he gives away are uniquely branded by him and can't be purchased anywhere in the world will definitely give him a leg up on sales. For the first time, Mr Toys products will be available to everyone, not just those on his list.

This guy must have a serious Santa complex. He probably even dresses the part, although I doubt he flies through the night sky on Christmas Eve with a bunch of reindeer pulling his sleigh. More than likely, he has a distribution centre in every major city on the planet and a fleet of trucks. Maybe even an entire transport company.

'Isobel?'

I jump at the sound of his voice and swing around in my seat, my hand bumping the table and sending my latte flying. He reaches past me and secures the cup before it can damage my laptop, and I am struck again by those sparkling blue eyes.

'Christian,' I manage to get out past the fog in my brain. 'What are you doing here?'

He lifts his cup. 'Coffee,' he says, sitting down at my table. 'What about you? Are you working?'

'Researching,' I say, shutting the lid of my computer and picking up my latte for a sip.

'So this isn't a vacation?'

'God no. My vacation was supposed to be in Bora Bora except my evil boss rescinded my vacation time and insisted I come here for a story.'

'Your head looks better.'

I shrug, blushing as I fiddle with my hair trying to keep the slowly decreasing lump on my head hidden. 'The swelling has gone down, and I covered the rest with makeup,' I say lamely.

He sips his coffee and seems to mull something over in his head. 'Do you have plans for the rest of the day?'

'No,' I shake my head and then kick myself. I shouldn't be hoping that he is going to ask me to spend the day with him.

'Have you ever been to New York before?'

'Uh-uh,' I shake my head again, getting lost in those hypnotic blue eyes.

'Spend the day with me. I'll show you around my favourite city.'

'New York is your favourite city?' I ask, surprised.

'It is. I especially like it in autumn, but winter can be pretty amazing too.'

'I hate winter,' I grumble, and he laughs.

'You hate winter and you hate Christmas,' he shakes his head. 'Let me try to change your mind about both.'

WHAT THE HELL am I doing? I really have no idea how I came to be holding Christian's hand while he drags me through the snowy streets of New York City. He's like a kid in a candy store, and I hate to admit that his enthusiasm is contagious. I even find myself laughing after nearly falling on my arse, from which he saves me. The guy is a menace.

'Are you warm enough?' he asks as a particularly bitter wind stirs up the snow flurries around us.

'I am,' I reply.

He stops to give me the once-over. 'Your luggage arrived.'

I shake my head. 'No, but I did spend an indecent amount of money at Macy's yesterday.'

He grins. 'It looks good on you.'

I flush with pleasure and hate myself for doing so. I am not that girl. I am not the one who seeks out compliments, who wants men to think she's pretty. I want to be known for my brain, not how good I look, but for some reason, knowing that Christian thinks I look good gives me tingles. I don't like it.

'Come on,' he says, pulling me along by the hand. 'We're going to miss it.'

'Where are you taking me?' I gasp as I try to keep up with his long-legged stride.

35

If he hadn't been holding my hand, I would have been left behind in the crowd, but Christian's sure steps keep us moving even when the crowded sidewalks come to a standstill. There is something commanding about him that causes people to get out of his way, but he is never rude and has a smile for every surly-faced New Yorker he passes.

He comes to a stop, and I run into his back. He grabs me and pulls me in front of him, his front to my back, wrapping his arms around my waist and leaning down to whisper in my ear.

'Wait for it.'

His hot breath causes me to shiver and involuntarily close my eyes with the thrill. I do not like the way my body responds to him. I do not like it at all.

The sound of carollers makes my eyes pop open, and I realise we are standing in front of Saks on 5$^{th}$ Avenue. Eight of the twelve windows are covered with heavy drapes, but the first four are on display—well, three are—the fourth one is just opening now as we watch. The familiar 'Twelve Days of Christmas' is being sung by real, live carollers who stand to the side of the window as the display is revealed. A crowd has gathered for the unveiling, and I allow myself to rest against Christian's chest, caught up in the moment. It feels nice to have his arms around me and his warm body behind me while we partake of a simple Christmas tradition. Lord knows, I've been involved in very few of those.

The window is finally uncovered, and it is stunning. A veritable forest is planted beyond the glass, with softly falling snow turning the scene into a winter wonderland. Each tree is wrapped in fairy lights, and the floor is covered in snow. It is beautiful, although I don't quite get the correlation with the song until the carollers fall quiet. One by one, four calling birds make themselves known, poking their heads out of the trees and singing sweetly. Each bird is different; each bird's song is different, and yet they blend beautifully.

'Wow,' I breathe.

I know the origins of the song, I know that originally the lyrics had been 'four colly birds', colly being the regional English for 'black', black birds, but I like the adapted version so much better after seeing it come to life. Four calling birds, each more lovely than the last, with a sweet song for the serenader's sweetheart.

'They reveal one window each day at this time,' he tells me.

'Like some sort of Advent Calendar?' I ask

He nods, 'Exactly like that.'

As the crowd begins to disperse, I turn to Christian. 'Can we look at the other windows?'

He smiles down at me and tucks a strand of hair behind my ear, his fingers lingering on my cheek. 'We can stay as long as you like.'

I look up at him and will him to kiss me. His eyes drop to my lips and I hold my breath, wanting to feel him pull me close, to wrap his arms around me and lower his head to mine. Someone bumps him from behind and the spell is broken. He smiles regretfully and then turns us towards the first window. I sigh and let the moment go, relieved and yet also disappointed.

The other windows are just as spectacular, my favourite being the partridge in the pear tree. They have a real pear tree in the window with plump, golden pears hanging from the branches. Okay, so maybe it isn't a real pear tree. What do I know? I've killed more plants than I have ever grown, but the effect is stunning. I don't know what a real partridge looks like, my only experience with the bird being the opening credits of the retro television show, The Partridge Family, so I am surprised to see the vibrant coloured bird perched on one of the tree limbs. I expected something more like a pheasant, but this bird does not have the long tail feathers or the sleek body. It is plump, with iridescent blue/green feathers covering its body and a bright red crest on its dark head. There is no real tail to speak of, but it is pretty just the same. Red-rimmed eyes follow me as I move close, its head tilting to the side to examine me. It can't possibly be real; it has to be motion-detection animatronics, but the effect is mesmerising. I feel a little like I'm in a fairy tale.

Okay, this isn't good. I'm losing my tough edge. When did I turn into a sentimental sap who falls for the cheap tricks of retailers trying to part me from my hard-earned cash? This will not do. I have to get away from it, clear my head, get back on track. I'm a journalist and a cynic. Sarcasm is my love language, not sissy purple prose.

'What's next?' I ask, turning from the window, desperate to resist its kitschy charm.

'Come with me,' Christian says, holding out his arm to me.

❄

'ICE SKATING?'

'It's a New York winter tradition.'

'But...ice skating?'

He laughs at what must be a horrified—no, make that terrified—look on my face. 'Come on, you'll be fine.'

'You have met me, right? In fact I do believe that you have seen me fall, trip and make a fool of myself enough times in the last few days to prove to you that me and ice skating should never go together.'

'Come on, Isobel,' he says, tugging my hand. 'How can you come to New York at Christmas and not ice skate in Central Park? That has to be some sort of crime.'

'But—'

'No more buts.'

'I don't know how—'

'I do and I won't let you fall.'

I bite my lip and look up at the sincerity in his eyes. My stomach is a jumble of nerves, but, for whatever reason, I give him my hand and let him drag me over to the skate hire. He hires our skates and then leads me over to a bench where we remove our shoes and put on our skates. He checks my laces to make sure they are tight enough and then stands, holding out his hand to me.

I hesitate. What's the worst that can happen? I could break my leg or my neck.

'Stop thinking and just do,' he says encouragingly and I scowl at him.

'Yes, Yoda,' I reply but take his proffered hand and allow him to help me to my feet.

The skates wobble beneath me as I try to walk, following him to the rink. I watch the hundreds of other people happily skating around on the ice. Children are doing it, for God's sake. I don't know why I'm afraid, but I can't help feeling that this is the worst idea in the world. I look up from the ice into Christian's eyes and the nerves in my stomach calm. There is something so strong and sure about him, something that makes me trust him. I don't know why, I don't trust easily, but he seems to be able to get passed all my defences.

I step out onto the ice with him and it feels like stepping off a cliff. My only lifeline is the large hand that envelopes mine. The large hand that is attached to the tall, blonde man with sparkling blue eyes. He smiles at me and I am lost. How did he get under my skin so quickly?

I grip his hands tightly as he leads me around the rink. Tiny children whizz by me making me feel like an idiot, but Christian's strong, steady reassurances keep me focussed. He is in front of me, skating backwards, pulling me along with him. I can't say that I am skating exactly, more like being dragged along, but I am still upright in a pair of ice skates on a frozen layer of ice. I'm ice skating and I dare anyone to say otherwise.

'See,' he says, a glint of mischief in his eyes. 'It's not so bad.'

'I guess,' I say.

My body is rigid, my knees locked, shoulders hunched, all in preparation of falling. It is inevitable that I will fall. I know it, my body knows it, and I'm pretty sure every other person on the ice knows it too. The only person who seems unconcerned is Christian.

He lets go of my hands briefly and I panic. He skates a circle around me while I stand there like a deer in headlights. He comes alongside me, putting one arm around my waist and taking my hand with his other one. He propels me along at a faster rate than we had been moving before, but with his warmth surrounding me, I start to relax, despite the danger and imminent fall that I know is coming.

'How about you try moving your feet,' he whispers in my ear and I shiver.

He shows me how to push off gently, one foot at a time. We go slow, but I can't stop the grin spreading across my face as the movement begins to feel more natural. We do a lap of the rink and the last of my tension falls away. I am nowhere near ready to go solo, but with Christian by my side, I feel ten times more confident than I did when I first laced up my skates. We manage a few more laps and, surprisingly, I'm having fun.

'Do you feel like some hot chocolate?' he asks as we near the gate where we entered the ice.

'That sounds wonderful,' I reply through chattering teeth.

He helps me off the ice and gets me situated on our bench. We remove our skates and he takes them back to the skate hire and comes back with two seeming cups of hot chocolate.

'See, that wasn't so bad, was it?'

I laugh, a genuine laugh. I feel light and breezy and relaxed for the first time in I don't know how long.

'No, that was actually kind of fun,' I say, bumping his shoulder gently.

He puts his arm around me and pulls me closer to him. It's nice, but I'm only doing it because I'm cold and I need his body heat to stop me from freezing my arse off.

'So you live in New York?' I ask into the comfortable silence that has descended on us.

'For about six months out of the year,' he says. 'I travel a lot for work.'

'And what is it that you do again?' I ask innocently.

He chuckles. 'Still haven't worked it out?'

I give him my best pout, but he just laughs.

'Come on,' he says, taking my empty cup and tossing it, with his, into the trash can. 'There's still more of New York I want you to see.'

He tugs me off the bench, and we hold hands as we walk back through the park. We wander the streets, dropping coins into the buckets of the Santas that seem to be on just about every corner. I gape like a typical tourist at the spectacle that is Times Square. I have seen it on television and in the movies, but that doesn't compare to what it's like in real life. We scope out the other Christmas window displays, and he buys me a warm soft pretzel from a street vendor. It's an amazing experience, seeing New York through Christian's eyes and, against my better judgement, I am enjoying myself.

'Hey,' I say, coming to a standstill in the middle of a busy sidewalk. 'What's that?'

Across the street is a large building shrouded in dark blue fabric. Along the front of the building stands four, two-storey tall toy soldiers like palace guards. Christian stands beside me and turns to look where I am pointing. He doesn't say anything for a long time and I turn to look at him. There is a really odd look on his face, but when he sees me watching him, he relaxes into a smile.

'It's a new toy store,' he replies. 'But they're not open yet.'

It has to be the Mr Toys toy store. I need to get a closer look. I step off the sidewalk, intent on getting across the street.

'Isobel, stop, wait!'

He grabs for me, but too late. My foot slips on the icy gutter, and I'm falling. I hear a screech of tires and a gasp from a passerby, and then I am on the ground looking up into a blue sky and wondering what the hell just happened.

WELL ISN'T this just the perfect way to end the most wonderful day I've ever had. Sitting in a backless hospital gown in a sterile room on a hard bed. My head hurts as does my ankle, which has swollen up to freaking cankle-like proportions.

Christian is waiting outside the examining room, and I feel so bad for ruining his day. I swear I'm never this clumsy, but right now I seem to be a one-woman natural disaster. I'm the manifestation of Murphy's Law. It's embarrassing.

'Isobel Carmichael?' a harried doctor says, coming into the room and not even looking up from his clipboard.

'Yes,' I say.

'Well, there's nothing broken. You're going to have a headache and a limp for a couple of days, but there is no major damage. I don't think you have a concussion, but I would feel better if you had someone stay with you tonight just to keep an eye on you and you will need to stay off that ankle and keep it elevated for at least the next twelve hours.'

'Okay,' I whimper.

'Do you have someone to stay with you?'

'I'll do it,' Christian says from the doorway.

'No, it's—'

'Excellent,' the doctor says, cutting me off. 'Here's a script for some pain meds which you can fill at the pharmacy just down the hall. Here's two for you to take now,' he hands me a small cup with two white pills and watches while I swallow them with a sip of water. 'And you're free to go. Sign here.'

I sign the release form and take the script and the doctor walks out.

'Christian, you don't have to—'

'Sh. I can and I will and I want to. Come on hop along, let's get you back to your hotel.'

'Um, I need to get dressed first.'

He blushes, 'Oh sure, okay. I'll just wait outside...'

I struggle to get my clothes back on, my head feeling a little woozy, but finally I manage it and call out to let Christian know I'm ready. He comes in and helps me into a wheel chair and pushes me out into the corridor.

'I paid your bill and got your script filled while you were dressing,' he says. 'So we can head straight back to the hotel.'

I just nod. My mouth feels like it is filled with cotton wool and I don't think I could speak even if I tried. He pushes me through the exit and there is a black car waiting for us. He helps me in and then slides in next to me. My eyes droop and I lean my head back against the soft seat. I'm really tired. The last thing I remember is his hand curling around mine as the car drives away.

# Day Five

*17<sup>th</sup> December*
*Unknown Hotel Suite, New York City*

I'm pretty sure I'm dead, and I'm okay with that. It's the only reasonable explanation I have for feeling like I am sleeping on a cloud. It's not just the feeling of sleeping on a cloud, there's also the fact that the air temperature is perfect. Not too hot, not too cold. Almost like I am one with the atmosphere and I can't tell where my skin begins and the air stops. And it's quiet, so wonderfully, blissfully, quiet.

I don't want to open my eyes in case it's all just a very elaborate dream. I don't know the last time I've slept so well and I'm content to just go on sleeping if I can prevent the onset of reality. I don't want reality right now, I want the dream, the place where it feels like everything good is happening to me, which I know for damned sure isn't my regular life.

But it's too late. My brain has switched on and that soft, happy feeling of a moment ago slowly seeps away as I become more aware of my surroundings. I haven't opened my eyes yet, but I know it's day time. I also know I'm alone, wherever I am. The responsible thing for me to do is open my eyes and find out just where that is, but I know that as soon as I do that, my dream will be over.

With a sigh I open my eyes and have to blink a couple of times before I can believe what I am seeing. The room is gorgeous, all plush furnishings and soft beiges. The curtains are closed, but I know that when I open them, I will have a spectacular view, probably of the park. The bed I am in is huge and I am snuggled into the middle of it like some sort of princess.

I try to sit up, but am reminded of last night's injuries when my head starts pounding. My mouth is dry, and I feel a little hung over, and then my ankle begins complaining, adding to the symphony of my woes. On the bedside table there are a long glass of water, a note and a pill bottle. I pick up the note to read:

> Good morning Isobel,
>
> This is now your room, apparently there was a mix up with your booking??
>
> I know you're probably feeling a little sore and sorry for yourself, so take the painkillers that the doctor prescribed, but perhaps take only one and make sure you eat! Last night you passed out on me and I think maybe the two pills the doctor gave you were too much, so just take one (but I'm not a doctor, so technically this isn't advice, just a friendly suggestion.)
>
> I had fun with you yesterday and I hope we can do it again sometime before you go home. I am working today, but if you need anything, here is my cell number. Call me anytime.
>
> Christian

I can't help smiling. I had a good time yesterday too, well, up until my spectacular fall from grace. I have never met someone like Christian, but then again, I socialise with mostly other journalists who are just as jaded as I am. There is no guile or hidden agenda with Christian, he is just a nice guy. My brain wants to tell me that there must be something wrong with him, no one can be that nice, he has to be hiding something. But for once, I don't want to listen to my brain, I want to listen to my heart and it's telling me that I can trust Christian.

With a self-indulgent sigh, I take a pill and swallow it down with some water. My stomach growls and I gingerly swing my legs over the side of the bed and limp into the living room. Yes, this is a suite, not just a pokey little studio like the one they originally stashed me in. Maryanne must have complained to them after my rant to her the other day and I am so very thankful for the upgrade.

The living area is just as opulent as the bedroom, and I limp over to the overstuffed couch, flopping down on it with a contented groan. I pick up the phone from the side table and order breakfast, my complaining stomach reminding me I have eaten nothing since the soft pretzel Christian bought me yesterday. The drapes in this room are open, and as I suspected earlier, there is a view of the park and the city skyline in the distance. This is the exact room that I imagined when I found out I was staying at Park Place, the one in all those romantic comedies that I watch.

Part of me is holding me back, waiting for the other shoe to drop. Good things rarely happen to me. Everything I have ever gotten has been because I worked freaking hard to make it happen. Nothing just drops in my lap, and there is a part of me that is suspicious of why I have suddenly been upgraded, not once but now twice. The upgrade to first class was also out of the blue, though at the time I was too grateful to be suspicious, but now...

I shake my head as there is a knock on my door. I am not going to ruin my good fortune by tempting fate. I am just going to accept this change in my luck, after all the bad luck I've had over the last few days aren't I due for something good to happen?

I hobble to the door and open it for the room service attendant. He wheels in my breakfast and I tip him generously, deciding it's good karma to share the wealth and then sit down to my feast. Anything could happen between now and when I have to leave, so I am going to enjoy this opportunity while I can. When will I ever have the chance again to live like the rich and famous? I may as well lap it up while I can and then I can leave New York with no regrets.

WHO KNEW that a shower such as this existed? Not me, that's for sure. This thing has six showerheads and one gigantic rainfall one. It's the best bloody shower I have ever had, and I want to stay there, under the warm water forever, but duty calls. I have to get to work on my article. So far I have zip, zero, zilch, and I am running out of time.

I dry off with the thickest towels I have ever seen and dress carefully. Being surrounded by such decadence has the unique influence on me to dress well and to maybe pretend for just a little while that living this way is my natural state. I even take time to do my makeup and blow out my hair. This is a big thing for me, especially with the tangled mess of curls that I was born with.

When I am suitably attired, I grab my laptop bag and head out the door, my ankle already feeling better. I discover I am on the sixteenth floor, not the penthouse, but close enough and I can't help smiling. I feel good today, better than I have felt in a long time. It's amazing what a good night's sleep will do, not to mention the company of a nice guy. I shake my head. My mood has nothing to do with Christian and everything to do with sleeping in the bed of luxury. He is just a nice side benefit.

He is gorgeous though. His sweet smile and sparkling blue eyes flash in my mind making me feel tingly all over. I really have to stop lying to myself about him, I can no longer deny the attraction. There is definitely something between us, but what can come of it? He lives here in New York City for six months of the year, the coldest six months too. There really can't be anything long term between us and I've just gotten out of a significant relationship. I need to be on my own for a while, get back the me that had been suffocating while I was with Michael.

Whoa, that's an interesting thought. Did I really feel suffocated by Michael? I know there were some things about me that he disapproved of and that I had endeavoured to change, but suffocated? Ultimately, I wasn't good enough for him, which meant all those changes were for nothing anyway. The more I think about it, the more I realise just how much I changed about myself to fit into his expectations and how little he changed for me. It was a relief when he called it off, I can admit that now. I thought I wanted to marry him, but really I just thought that it was time I got married and he was the closest thing to an eligible candidate. That is a really depressing realisation.

The elevator doors open on the lobby, interrupting my train of thought. I pushed those thoughts to the back of my mind and walked, as normally as I can on my bum ankle, towards the front desk.

'Ms Carmichael,' the clerk says. 'I hope you room is to your liking.'

'Yes,' I reply, nodding. 'It's wonderful.'

'On behalf of Park Place, I must apologise for the mix up with your room and let you know that the rest of your stay will be free of charge.'

I feel my eyebrows pop up at that, but I will not look a gift horse in the mouth. 'Thank you,' I reply with as much decorum as I can manage. 'Do you know if the airline has located my luggage yet?'

He taps some keys on the computer and frowns. 'Unfortunately not yet. But there is an envelope for you.'

He turns to retrieve the envelope from a pigeon hole behind him and hands it to me. It is a thick creamy paper with my name written in a beautiful script across the front.

'Thank you,' I say in a daze, turning to find a chair to sit down on while I open the note.

> *My dearest Isobel,*
>
> *I know I should probably leave you alone and let you get to the work that brought you to the city, but I can't seem to. Have dinner with me tonight, let me see you just one more time.*
>
> *I'll send a car for you at seven. If you can't make it, please let the concierge know, but I'm hoping you will say yes.*
>
> *Christian*

This guy is just too much and a little thrill of excitement runs through me at the thought of dinner with him. How can I turn down such a sweet invitation? And if I do some work today then I can justify a night off with a gorgeous man. Maryanne wouldn't begrudge me that.

I giggle. Seriously, me, giggling. What is this guy doing to me? Where is the no-holds-barred, tough-as-nails reporter that left Sydney with a bad attitude and a chip on her shoulder? I'm even starting to like New York City and freaking snow. Me, a self-confessed sun worshipper is able to see the beauty of the soft snow flakes as they blanket the city and turn everything into a picture perfect postcard.

Hanging out with Christian is bad for me. He's making me soft and I just can't afford to be soft in my profession. Journalism is a tough gig for those of us who want to do the serious stuff and I have worked long and hard to prove to the grouchy old-school reporters that I am every bit as hard-nosed as they are, but four days in Christian's presence and I'm turning into some sappy girl with hearts in her eyes. Next I'll be skipping down the side walk and bursting into song. I really should stay away from him, for my own preservation.

But I can't. I feel myself yearning to see him just one more time; to see his smile, feel his hand in mine and maybe, feel his lips on mine. If I'm honest with myself, I've wanted him to kiss me from the first moment I set eyes on him in the middle of Sydney airport. I wonder if I will finally get my wish tonight?

I shake my head to clear it. I've got a few hours to fill until tonight and I really need to get some work done. With a sigh, I stand and sling my laptop bag over my shoulder and limp towards the door. I'll find a coffee shop with some free wifi and settle in for a good, long stretch of investigative journalism, you know, the reason I'm actually in this godforsaken place. I'm not here for the pretty man with his sparkling blue eyes and toothpaste advertising smile. I'm here to work.

THE RESTAURANT IS like nothing I have ever seen before. Housed in the iconic, art déco Metropolitan Life North Building opposite Madison Square Park, Eleven Madison Park was a three Michelin star restaurant, the calibre of which I have never experienced. I have to physically clench my jaw to stop my mouth from falling open as I gaze around the gorgeous interior with its high ceilings and tall, muntin windows. Enormous foliage displays are placed strategically around the room, and large, white-clothed tables hold a sparkling array of crystal wine glasses and polished silver flatware.

We are shown to an intimate table with a view of the park, and I feel completely out of my depth. Christian smiles brightly at me, calming me enough that I can take in the entire atmosphere without embarrassing myself. I look at the man sitting opposite me and wonder once more who he is. This place can't be cheap, and he is always immaculately dressed in bespoke suits, which he wears with all the ease as if they were well-worn jeans and a t-shirt.

'Have I impressed you?' he asks and I smile at his cheeky grin.

'You have,' I say before glancing around the room once more. 'This place is gorgeous.'

'It pales in comparison to you,' he says softly and I feel my cheeks heat with a girlish blush.

We share a quiet moment before a waiter approaches and explains the coming tasting meal. Eight courses of seasonal and local produce, including some share plates as well as individual offerings. The waiter then hands Christian the wine list for his perusal and leaves us alone.

'Is there a particular wine you like?' he asks looking up at me and offering me the menu.

I shake my head. My wine knowledge is limited to what is on sale at the local liquor store. 'I'm sure whatever you pick will be perfect.'

'Do you even like wine?' he asks and I chuckle.

'I do. Although I am not all that experienced with it.'

'Well, then,' he says, snapping the menu shut. 'Tonight I am going to ruin you for regular wine.'

'I like the sound of that,' I say.

When we are approached by the sommelier, Christian orders a complicated French-sounding wine, and the sommelier nods and exits with a 'very good, sir'.

'Have I changed your mind about New York City?' he asks after we have been served our wine.

I smile and tilt my head. 'Is that what you were trying to do?'

'I thought it was obvious.'

I chuckle. 'It has grown on me. I'm even warming up to snow...if that makes any sense at all.'

He laughs and the warm sound flows over me like the gentle caress of a summer breeze. Oh, this man is dangerous, more dangerous than I realised.

'So why are you here in The Big Apple? I know you're working on something...'

I take a sip of wine and suppress the moan of delight that wants to escape my lips. I close my eyes to savour the taste and when I open them, Christian is looking at me hungrily, his eyes dark and intense. I swallow and try to control the rapid beat of my pulse as I try to remember what it was he asked me.

I clear my throat and attempt to clear my head. 'Um, my boss, Maryanne, wants me to do a story on a reclusive billionaire.'

His eyebrows rise. 'That's not the type of piece you normally do,' he says, and it is my turn to be surprised.

'You Googled me,' I say and he flushes and drops his eyes.

'You intrigued me,' he says, raising his eyes to me again. 'Especially when I found out that you write for Iconoclast. It's one of my favourite magazines and, as I discovered after my Google search, you are one of my favourite writers.'

My cheeks flush with pleasure. Iconoclast is a small news magazine that is more often than not hated by the establishment for its mandate not to pander to the rich and powerful. I had seen the decline of unbiased reporting over the years and the propensity for journalists to grab the low-hanging fruit instead of discovering the real story. Too much of today's reporting was about getting the soundbite, and to me that wasn't real reporting at all but sensationalising for the sake of a report that might go viral. Iconoclast had set out to be different, and because of that, we weren't exactly a favourite among people like Christian.

'Really?' I ask.

'The piece you did on the seemingly revolving door of Australian Prime Ministers was brilliant.'

A grin split my face, and I couldn't stop it, not that I wanted to. 'I am very proud of that piece. Although I received some nasty fan mail afterwards.'

'If you're not upsetting someone, then you're not doing it right.'

A surprised laugh comes out of my mouth. 'I can't imagine you upsetting anyone,' I say.

He frowns. 'You still haven't worked out who I am, have you?'

I shake my head. 'I don't think I want to,' I say softly. 'I like the man I have come to know, not whatever your reputation has to say about you.'

His eyes soften at my words and I wonder what it is that he's worried about me finding out.

We walk hand in hand under fairy lights that wind around the avenue of trees through the park. I don't know if it's the wine or just being with him, but I'm feeling a bone-deep contentment. I like who I am when I am with him. He's seen me at my worst, and I don't feel like I have to pretend around him. There are no masks, and I get the feeling that even if there were, he would see right through them.

Dinner was amazing. My tastebuds are still dancing from the tantalising flavours and I know I will never experience anything quite like that again. This whole night has developed a dream-like quality, the edges of which are soft and fuzzy. It feels like we are the only two in the universe as we meander through the softly falling snow. He leads me under an archway and stops, turning to face me.

I look up at him and my pulse begins to gallop. This is it, this is the moment. He looks up and I follow his gaze, noticing the bunch of waxy green leaves and white flowers.

'Mistletoe,' he whispers before lowering his mouth to mine.

The first brush of his kiss is tender and I melt into him. His lips slide across mine, the pressure increasing as he winds his arms around me and pulls me closer. I reach up and entwine my hands behind his neck, pulling his head down to mine and opening my lips to him, inviting him in. He deepens the kiss and I can feel it all the way down to my toes. He doesn't rush. He takes his time as he explores my mouth and I can feel important parts of my body coming alive as I press myself against him. There are too many clothes between us; bulky jackets and scarves that are keeping the cold off us, but preventing us from getting as close as we would really like to be.

One of his hands is in my hair, cupping the back of my head as the other one spans my lower back. His lips are soft and I can taste the wine and chocolate from desert on his tongue. I am surrounded by his scent, cinnamon and spice and that underlying smell that is uniquely his. I could stay here, wrapped in his embrace forever and I feel myself falling.

He lifts his head first and looks down at me with heavy lids.

'I have been wanting to do that for the longest time,' he says.

'Me too,' I whisper in reply and the side of his mouth quirks up in a crooked smile.

His hand traces my cheek and jaw, his thumb rubs across my bottom lip and I see something in his eyes that I don't understand.

'What am I going to do with you Izzy?' he murmurs before lowering his head to mine once again and capturing my lips in a searing kiss.

I usually hate to be called Izzy, but coming from him, it sounds like an endearment and I don't mind at all. It is a tad ironic that he has a nickname for me when his own mother is so dead against them, but what do I care? This man with his sweet smile and gentle ways has barrelled through every one of my road blocks and I know that I am in danger of becoming irrevocably entangled with him.

# Day Six

*18th December*
*Park Place, New York City*

I'm singing in the shower and am ridiculously happy. It's pathetic really. I can't believe I've turned into that girl, but I can't really muster much righteous anger about it, I'm too bloody happy.

I couldn't have imagined a better date. The more time I spend with that incredible man, the more I crave it. I nearly did the unthinkable last night and invited him to my room, but he stopped me by kissing me goodnight and getting back in his car, leaving me alone on the steps of the hotel. I didn't know whether to be relieved or to feel rejected.

But how can I be upset with a guy who treats me so well? I've always poo-poohed the whole chivalry hullabaloo, but after experiencing it firsthand, I have to confess that I like it. Not once did he make me feel powerless or less than. Instead, he made me feel cherished.

God, listen to me. I'm freaking pathetic. When did I turn into a simpering Disney princess? I don't do romance. I don't do sweet unless it's to get something I want. Christian is ruining me... but in the best way.

No.

I need to keep my eye on the ball. There are only six days left for me to get my expose on Mr Toys, and so far I've got nothing.

I get out of the shower and dress, forgoing the makeup and the hairdryer. I need to slip back into Isobel Carmichael, hard-headed reporter for Iconoclast, and leave this other sweet, smiling, *singing* Izzy behind. Today I will find something. I have to.

I set myself up at the desk with my laptop and start scouring the web for something, anything, that will give me a clue about who this guy is. I click on a picture of a toy train. It is well made and looks durable. You can't buy anything else like it in normal stores. I nibble my thumb as I think that over. All the toys delivered by Mr Toys are made especially for him, for his deliveries. These are not mass-produced junk that breaks after a few weeks. These are made with an eye for detail and a distinct quality. How does he produce them? Does he commission factories to make them, or does he have his own factories? And if he has his own factories, why has no one ever spilled the beans as to his operation?

The more I research this guy, the more intrigued I get. He's set himself up as some mystical being that makes toys and delivers them to kids all over the world. The parallels to the story of a mythical Santa Claus are not lost on me. Maybe that was the intention all along. But why? And how could he possibly keep doing it all these years later? He has to be dead by now or a very old man...perhaps there is a new guy in town, a legacy Mr Toys.

But that doesn't help me at all. How can I possibly track down a legacy when I have no clue who the original is? No, the toys are the key. If I can find out more about the toys, then maybe I can trace them back to the man. I have to get inside that toy store. It is opening in six days, so surely they would be stocking the shelves inside, and if I could get in there, I might find out just where those toys are coming from.

With renewed energy, I jump up and grab my purse and coat. I didn't see any security near the building the other day when we were there, and there has to be a back door or a delivery entrance. The toys are surely being shipped in on trucks. There is no way all of those toys could have been made onsite.

Before I can leave the suite, there is a knock at my door. I open it to discover a bellboy and my suitcase.

'Ms Carmichael?' he asks hesitantly.

'Yes?'

'Your luggage arrived this morning.'

I look down at the suitcase. The poor thing has seen better days, and by the amount of tags attached to it, it has had quite a journey.

'Thank you. You can put it in the bedroom.'

The bellboy deposits my bag in the room, and I tip him on the way out.

'Hey,' I call to him before he disappears down the hall.

He turns to me. 'Yes, ma'am, is there something else I can do for you?'

'Just a question. What do you know about Mr Toys and the store he's opening?'

His face creases in a smile, and I notice just how young he is. 'Mr Toys is a legend. I got a gift from him once, when I was a kid.'

'Really?' I ask, my eyebrows rising.

He flushes and nods. 'I grew up in and out of foster homes,' he says quietly. 'One Christmas I was in a group home. The holidays are the worst time to be taken in by a family. Anyway, none of us were too happy to be there, but on Christmas morning when we woke up, the communal living area had been decorated with all sorts of Christmas decorations and there was an enormous tree surrounded by gifts with our names on them. He'd also provided a feast of food for us, roast turkey and ham and all the trimmings. It was the best day of my life.'

'What was your gift?' I ask.

'A telescope. I used to climb out onto the roof and look at the stars at night. I'd spend hours in the library looking up anything and everything I could about astronomy. That telescope changed my life.'

'How?'

He ducks his head and blushes furiously. 'I'm studying Astrophysics and I never would have even known what it was without that telescope.' He clears his throat. 'Will there be anything else, ma'am?'

I shake my head and let him go. How did Mr Toys know this boy needed a telescope? Or was it just dumb luck?

❄

STANDING outside the toy store that is shrouded in mystery is impressive. The supersize toy soldiers are quite a sight with their brightly coloured blue and red uniforms. I am not the only gawker, and many jaded New Yorkers stop and stare at the huge wooden toys.

I turn to one guy. 'What do you think about this store opening?' I ask.

He shrugs. 'The last thing we need is another toy store, but my niece got a job there, and she's a single mom who's been out of work for a while, so I suppose that's a good thing.'

'I think it's great,' another bystander says. 'It'll be nice to shop in a store that has something different.'

'It's going to be expensive, though,' someone else says. 'Have you seen the toys this guy makes? I'll be lucky if I can afford a keychain from the place.'

'Yeah, but this guy gives his toys away, so why would he charge exorbitant prices for them?'

'He's gotta make his money somehow.'

A crowd has gathered around me, giving me their opinions of the store. It's great. I feel like I'm in my element. These people are being honest, and not everyone is happy about the store opening, although there are fewer of those and more of the ones who are impressed about the jobs that have been made available.

'What do you know about the guy, Mr Toys?' I throw out the question to the group.

'He's gotta be a sandwich or two short of a picnic, doesn't he?' one guy says. 'Why else would he give away so many toys every year?'

'I think he's more like Willy Wonka,' a woman says. 'I think he's lonely, and making children smile makes him feel good.'

'It's probably a tax write-off,' another person says. 'It can't be his main company. He probably owns a huge multinational and needs to lower the taxes he pays.'

'I disagree. I think he does it because he knows what it's like to be poor, and now that he's made his millions, he wants to give back.'

'Do you have any theories about who he really is?' I ask.

'Bezos,' someone says, and the crowd laughs.

'No way is it Bezos. That guy wouldn't know the first thing about giving back.'

'I don't think it's just one guy,' a voice says, 'I think it's a whole team of people, maybe like a Mastermind group and they are all high-powered businessmen with squillions of dollars and they each donate towards the cause.'

'I think it's a woman,' a female voice says. 'There's no way a guy does all this.'

Snow starts falling, and the crowd disperses, leaving me standing there looking up at the building with its dark blue covering and wondering just what mysteries are hidden beneath. With a quick look around to make sure no one is watching me, I slip down the narrow alley beside the building. It's deserted and surprisingly clean. I head for the first door I see and press the handle, but it's locked. I move down to the next one and try it, but again it's locked. Before I can get to the next one, it opens and a young guy walks out, lighting up a cigarette. I duck into a doorway to hide, but he sees me.

'Hey, what are you doing here? This is a restricted area.'

'I ah,' I look around helplessly. 'I'm lost.'

'Freaking tourists,' he growls. 'You need to leave. You're not allowed to be here.'

He tosses his cigarette on the ground as I turn around, but as soon as he walks back inside, I make a beeline for the door and grab it just before it closes. I peek around the door into a dark corridor and then check behind me to make sure no one can see me as I slip through the opening and let the door close softly behind me. It takes a moment for my eyes to adjust to the dimness, and then I slink down the hallway. I pass closed and locked doors on the way, but then as I round a corner I see light up ahead and I can hear voices. I creep towards the end of the corridor and sneak a look out into the light.

The toy shop floor is something out of a storybook or a kid's dream. There is so much to see that I don't know where to look first. Brightly coloured kites hang from the ceiling; toy planes whir in circles on almost invisible wires. There is a giant hot-air balloon sculpture in one corner, and the basket is overflowing with balls of every colour and size. An entire wall of shelves is filled with soft toys of every shape and size. I am so overwhelmed by it all that I step into the light, not caring who sees me.

Workers of varying nationalities wearing a rainbow of coloured uniforms are scurrying around unpacking boxes and stocking shelves. There is an atmosphere of joy, and the staff chat and laugh as they go about their chores. A beach ball rolls towards me, having escaped from a display that a young guy is setting up, and I bend down to pick it up. It looks just like the one I used to have when I was a kid, the segments of red, blue, green and yellow. I remember playing on the beach with it for several summers in a row. God, I loved that thing. It was just a stupid plastic ball, but it embodied school holidays and summer vacation. I made my dad patch it a couple of times when it had been punctured, and then one year my mother demanded it as part of her twisted sacrifice. It was just a stupid ball, but I cried as I watched it burn in the backyard incinerator. My dad had offered to buy me a new one later that night after my mother had retired to her room, but the damage had been done. I hadn't played with one since.

'Isobel?'

I looked up from the ball to see Christian.

'Are you crying?'

I DROP the ball and wipe my face, surprised to find tears on my cheeks. I can't remember the last time I cried over something my mother had done, I thought I'd grown out of it. I shake myself and straighten my shoulders.

'Christian,' I say, thankful that my voice is steady. 'What are you doing here?'

'I could ask you the same question,' he says his head cocked. 'How did you get in?'

I point vaguely behind me, 'The door was open,' I hedge.

His lips thin and his jaw clenches. In all the time I have spent with him, I have never seen him angry or even mildly upset. The man standing in front of me is not the same man I know.

'You make a habit of just walking through unlocked doors on a whim?' he asks, his voice a controlled growl.

'No,' I say weakly. 'I was curious about the store—'

'You need to leave,' he says through gritted teeth. 'Now.'

'Wait, hang on,' I say as he herds me off the shop floor. 'Why are you here? What have you got to do with this store?'

He doesn't answer me as he continues to shepherd me down the corridor toward the door to the alley.

'Christian, answer me,' I say as he opens the door and pushes me out into the alley. Anger is rolling off him in waves, and I'm shocked by his show of temper.

'You can't be here,' he says, his eyes no longer sparkling, but glinting like cold blue sapphires.

'But you can?' My anger is rising at his treatment of me. It's not the first time I've been tossed out on my arse, but it's the first time it's hurt so much. Not physically hurt, but hurt because I thought I knew this man and I thought there were no secrets between us, which is a stupid thing to think because we'd only known each other for six days.

'You are a member of the press,' he says, his anger cooling off a touch. 'And we have a press embargo in place until the opening of the store.'

'So this is because I'm a journalist?' I ask.

His brow furrows in confusion. 'Of course that's what it's about. What else could it be?'

The insecurity I feel is a revelation to me. Never before have I been so unsure around another person, man or woman. I like this guy and I want him to like me back and the fact that he just tossed me out of a store he obviously has some connection to makes me doubt his feelings for me.

'I, uh, I don't know. I thought maybe it was about last night.'

His face softens, and the anger is replaced with something else entirely. He steps towards me and takes me in his arms, dipping his head to place a soft kiss on my lips.

'I'm sorry,' he says, nuzzling my nose. 'I overreacted to seeing you here. I thought...'

'What?' I ask, looking up at him. 'What did you think?'

He shakes his head. 'It doesn't matter. It's stupid. I'm sorry for being such a bastard. Forgive me?'

'On one condition,' I say and his brow furrows. 'Kiss me.'

He smiles, and the sparkle is back in his eye as he lowers his head and whispers against my lips, 'Your wish is my command.'

His kiss is hot and sweet and I forget for a minute where we are. I could get lost in this man, I could forget my own name when he touches me. My bones melt as I press myself against him and it is with great reluctance that I let his mouth go when he lifts his head. He tucks a curl behind my ear and the look he gives me is so full of meaning that I feel like I'm drowning in it.

I claw back some of my sanity and search his eyes. I want to ask him why he is here, but I don't want to cause a rift between us. The conflicted feeling about asking a question is new. Asking the hard questions is what I'm all about. But asking Christian what connection he has to Mr Toys and Toyland is turning my insides out.

'I'm consulting on the store layout,' he says, reading me better than anyone else has in my entire life. 'I was contracted to make sure that the flow of the floor is optimal for customer interaction.'

I let out a breath I was holding. 'Thank you. You didn't have to tell me that.'

He shrugs a shoulder. 'I know. But I wanted to. It's my way of apologising for getting mad at you before.'

I pat his chest with one of my gloved hands. 'You're a good man, Christian Palmer.'

His smile falters a bit, but he kisses me one last time and then steps back towards the door. 'I wish we could continue this,' he says, with a mischievous look in his eye. 'But I do have to get back to work.'

'Will I see you later?' I ask hopefully.

He looks at his watch and then back over his shoulder before looking back at me with regret in his eyes. He shakes his head. 'No, not tonight. I'll be here until well after midnight. Can I call you tomorrow?'

I smile through my disappointment. 'Sure,' I say. 'Wait, do you have my number?'

We exchange numbers and then he gives me another quick kiss before disappearing back into the store. I touch my lips with my fingers and then shake my head in disgust. I really am losing my edge. I seem to turn into some sort of silly, starstruck girl whenever I'm around that man. I need to get a grip, I've got a story to write.

# Day Seven

I shouldn't feel so guilty doing this, but I do. I tossed and turned most of the night, hardly getting a wink of sleep, mulling over what I had discovered yesterday. Christian was my passport to find Mr Toys. I have never felt bad about using my connections to get close to the people I write about, but this time it feels wrong; it feels like a betrayal.

But this is my job, and I have a story due in five days, and so far I've got nothing but a couple of statements from unknown people, conflicting statements at that. The bellboy who delivered my luggage had more information on the man I'm trying to find than I did. It is a blow to my ego and a slight to my professional reputation. I have never failed to get a story in on time before, and I have never failed to find my mark, however hidden they were.

So now I'm in a taxi following Christian's limousine like some bad PI movie. I was at Starbucks, drowning my sorrows with caffeine when I saw him come in. He didn't see me and the idea to follow him just struck me. Christian may not know the man, Mr Toys, himself, but he was a hell of a lot closer to him than I was at the moment, so he was my only hope.

Except that it feels wrong and my gut is tied up in knots about my subterfuge. Maybe if I just talked to him, asked him to get me in... but no. What if he says no? Then I've ruined this winter fling we have going and I don't get my story either. Following him covertly is my only hope at this stage. And if I do it right, he will never find out.

The limo pulls over and Christian steps out, entering a tall bronze and glass building. The cabby finds a spot to park and turns to me.

'What is this building?' I ask.

'The Seagram Building,' he replies.

'Any interesting businesses inside?' I ask and he shrugs.

'No one I know.'

We wait in silence. The limousine is still parked out front, which makes me think Christian won't be inside for very long. I made a deal with the cab driver to hire him for the day. He seems to like the intrigue of following a rich guy around.

I pull out my phone and do a quick internet search on the building. Investment, private equity and banking firms make up the tenants of the building. Money men. Does one of these firms finance Mr Toys? Or do they have something to do with Christian's own business? It is so tempting to Google the man, but the challenge he laid down stops me. I am not a cheater, even when I am dying of curiosity. There's also a small part of me that doesn't want to discover a dirty little secret about him. I like him and his Prince Charming persona; I'm not ready to see it dragged through the mud.

His tall, blonde head emerges from the building and slides into the backseat of the limousine. The cabby puts his newspaper away and pulls out into the traffic behind the sleek black car. We travel through the stop start traffic until we lose the limo to a private underground parking garage. The taxi does the block.

'What do you want me to do?' he asks.

I twist and turn in my seat trying to see what building it is that Christian has disappeared into. It looks like a department store.

'Find a place to park,' I say.' I'm going to go in and see if I can find him.'

The cabby nods and pulls across a couple of lanes of traffic to a cacophony of blaring horns and parks in a loading zone.

'I'll be as quick as I can,' I say, opening the door.

'Take your time,' he says with a grin, opening up his newspaper again. 'The meter is running.'

I jump out of the cab and weave through the slow-moving traffic, arriving on the opposite sidewalk without damage. I look up at the building and see a familiar logo. Hayden Bros. They're an Australian company, a high-end department store that has been expanding its reach by opening stores in other major cities across the globe. I had no idea they had one in New York City.

I walk through the doors and take in the shiny glass and polished marble. This has to be at least five steps up from the store in Sydney, the only other Hayden's that I've been in.

The first floor is perfume and makeup, which seems to be a pretty standard layout for every department store I have ever been in. Well-dressed women manning the cosmetic counters look down their collective noses at me as I wander through. I think they can tell that I don't have the money to shop here, but it's a free country and there's no sign saying I can't browse. Besides, haven't they seen Pretty Woman? How do they know I don't have a billionaire silver fox as a sugar daddy? Or better yet, how do they know I'm not the billionaire? It'd be their loss if I were.

I look up at the glittering chandelier that probably costs more than I could earn in five years, and my eyes connect with his. He is standing on the floor above, speaking to a stuffy-looking man who is holding a clipboard and talking animatedly. I see the moment he sees me, the surprise which is replaced with pleasure and then suspicion. That's my cue to leave. I turn on my heel and make my way back through the perfume counters, doing my best to avoid the evil women with their spray bottles.

I break through the front door and take a breath of fresh air before getting my bearings and looking for my cab.

'Isobel!'

His voice calling my name spurs me into action, and I make a run for it. I dodge pedestrians and cars like a pro, sliding into the backseat of my cab before Christian can catch me.

'Go, go, go!' I yell at the cabby, and he tears away from the curb, tires squealing.

I lean back in my seat and take some slow, measured breaths, trying to calm my racing heart.

WE MAKE it back to Park Place unscathed, and I hand over the money with a generous tip. I scurry into the lobby and keep my head down. I don't know if Christian will follow me here, or if he was able to beat me back here, but if he has, I want to avoid him at all costs.

I know I will have to face him eventually. He is going to want an explanation for why I was following him and why I ran. It looked suspicious as hell, but I panicked. I was thrown by the store, the opulence and exclusivity that I have never experienced before. Hayden Bros is well known as the most expensive store in Australia, but the store here in New York made the Sydney store look like a run-of-the-mill suburban K-Mart.

And why was Christian there? Why was he talking to, who I presume to be, the store manager?

I gratefully make it through my suite door without having to make eye contact with anyone. I drop my bag and remove my coat as I mull over the enigma that is Christian Palmer. The first time I met him, I thought he was a flake, a rich playboy with nothing better to do than torture me. The more I get to know him, the less that image fits him.

I can no longer deny that I have feelings for the man. Big, messy, complicated feelings. Feelings that are dangerous for someone like me, feelings that have already interfered with my doing my job. I can't afford to fall for him. I can't afford to let anything distract me from the job I was sent here to do.

'Freaking hell!' I yell at the universe. Why is this happening to me? The timing sucks the big one. Why couldn't I have met Christian at another time, another place? Why couldn't we have met when I wasn't on the trail to reveal who his very mysterious boss is? Why did we have to be on opposite sides of this.

A knock at my door makes me jump. I know who it is, even without looking. I can tell by the angry knock and my body is already reacting to his nearness.

'Let me in Isobel,' he yells through the door.

I'm frozen where I stand. If I don't let him in then I don't have to deal with the fallout of falling for someone I can never have. If I don't let him in, I can hold on to the fantasy a little bit longer.

'Come on, Izzy,' he says, his voice lower this time. 'Let me in. We need to talk.'

It's the nickname that gets to me. The fact that he's using it means that maybe not all is lost. My feet take me across the room and I open the door. He stands there in all his male glory and the power and authority radiating off him is like a drug.

'Can I come in?'

I step back, opening the door wider so he can enter the room. His body brushes mine as he slides past and I have to hold back a groan. This is really not the time to be thinking bedroom thoughts, but there is just something about this man that affects me in a very visceral way.

I close the door and stand there waiting for him to yell at me. He paces the room, one hand in his pants pocket, the other raking through his hair and making it stand up at crazy angles. His silence is ratcheting up the tension in my body until I am practically vibrating with it.

'You were following me,' he says. It's not a question.

I nod.

'How long? How long have you been following me? This thing between us, is this all some sort of way for you to get a story on me?'

'No! God no, never. I wouldn't do that.' I can't believe he would think that about me, and it raises the question of why he would think that. Why would he think I wanted to do a story about him? Who is this guy?

'Really?' he asks, disbelief and disappointment dripping from the words.

I take a step closer to him. 'Really,' I say softly.

'So why? Why are you following me?'

I bite my lip, not sure how much to tell him.

'Don't lie to me, Isobel.'

'I only followed you today,' I admit.

'And yesterday?'

'That was pure, dumb luck,' I say.

'What were you really doing at Toyland yesterday?'

The one question I didn't want to answer, but did I have a choice?

'You know how I told you I was doing a story on a reclusive billionaire—'

'Mr Toys,' he says with a sigh, dropping his head and rubbing the back of his neck. 'You're here to do a story on Mr Toys.'

I nod, my bottom lip caught between my teeth. 'I didn't know you worked for him, I swear, not until yesterday.'

'And so today? Why were you following me?'

I look at the ground, ashamed of what I'd done. He steps closer to me and lifted my chin with his index finger.

'I thought you could lead me to him.'

A look very much like relief crosses his face before being replaced with anger. 'You didn't think to just ask me?'

'It was a spur of the moment—'

'What you just saw me and decided to tail me all day?'

'Well—' I look away again, not able to face the look in his eyes.

'Dammit Izzy,' he growls, threading his hands through my hair and tilting my head so I can't look away from him again. 'What the hell am I going to do with you?'

He slams his mouth against mine in an angry, hungry kiss and my body goes into meltdown. This. This is exactly what he can do to me. I give him my blessing to do this and more.

CLOTHES ARE REMOVED MAKING a trail leading to the bedroom. His mouth is hot on mine, barely letting me up to breathe, not that I care. Who needs to breathe when I can die kissing him?

We collapse on the bed in a tangle of naked arms and legs, our bodies twining together, neither one of us wanting to be parted from the other. I know he's angry with me, I'm angry too, but I'd much rather work out our differences with a little naked wrestling than yelling and tears and hurtful words that can't be taken back. Our bodies know and sometimes it's better to let our bodies do the talking instead of our brains.

I'm no slouch in the bedroom department, but with Christian everything seems to be heightened. My skin is on fire from his touches, from his kisses and I can't get enough of him. I don't want this night to end until I know every inch of him and he knows every inch of me.

It's hard and fast; at times brutal and other times tender. He owns me completely, ruining me for any other man. I know I will walk away from this encounter changed. He is demolishing every carefully constructed wall around my heart and soul with each kiss and caress. I am helpless under his sensual assault, but I'm not afraid. He is stripping me bare, and for the first time in my life, I am comfortable being vulnerable. I welcome it even.

Hearts beating in tandem, our very souls connecting as our bodies peak and then free fall, tethers broken until it's just the two of us in a universe of our own. Nothing held back, nothing hidden, and in this moment... I know. It's too fast, it's too big, but I can't deny it. I have fallen in love with this man, and there is absolutely nothing I can do about it.

Later, we lay together in each other's arms. There are no words, there is no need for them. Words would only complicate what we have discovered in each other. I'm happy just to be held securely in his arms, his touch holding me together, preventing me from falling apart. We are both changed and now we need to navigate the new normal that we find ourselves in.

I'm not naive enough to think that there won't be something to answer for in the morning, but for now, it's just the two of us and this new truth. Real life will come soon enough, but for this moment in time I can pretend that the path ahead is clear of obstacles. The questions of where we go from here are stuffed back in a box that I will open later. I don't want anything to ruin this perfect moment.

I turn my head to look up at him. He is watching me with a look a lot like love. The same look is reflected in my gaze. I hide my face in the crook of his neck, and his hand tangles in my unruly curls, holding me close. He feels it too. I know he understands that this moment is too big to understand.

He rolls us over so that he is holding himself over me, looking down at me, searching my gaze. I don't know what he's looking for, but I don't hide anything from him, not tonight. Tomorrow will come soon enough and bring with it all the unanswered questions and withheld secrets. But for right now, I want him to see my heart, to gaze upon my very soul.

He kisses me. It's slow and languid and the worries that had begun to gather are silenced as he ministers to me with his tongue and lips. My need for him, which I thought fulfilled only minutes ago, is hungry and demanding. He knows, and responds in kind. It's like we have been together for eternity and our bodies know what the other needs. There is no need for words, no need for grasping or groping in the dark. Every touch, every caress, every nip and sip and kiss is a choreographed dance that the two of us know intimately.

There is no anger this time, no demands, no need for retribution. It's slow and sweet and tender, but it's also deep and intense and meaningful. There is heat, but not the flash bang of earlier, this heat is a slow burn and it goes far deeper than I ever thought possible.

Every moment with Christian is a revelation. He always manages to peel back my layers and reveal my soft underbelly. I've never let anyone this close before, never trusted anyone enough to see beneath my armour, but I am defenceless when it comes to this man. He has complete access to every part of me and I open to him willingly. What should be frightening, feels natural and I know that my secrets are safe with him.

The contentment I feel as he holds me close is all consuming. I could go to sleep every night with his arms around me and wake every morning the same. A future with this man seems possible, inevitable even. I want the fantasy life that scrolls like a movie montage through my head as his hands caress me and our breathing evens out.

I hear his heart beating as I rest my head on his chest, I hear his breath and feel the warmth of his skin. I can smell the spicy cinnamon scent of his aftershave and his taste is on my lips. My world narrows down to my five senses, all of which are filled with this man that I love.

'Izzy,' he breathes, the sound of his voice resonating in his chest with a comforting rumble. 'My Izzy.'

He speaks the truth. I am his and he is mine. It is an undeniable truth, irrefutable and unchangeable. Whatever comes next, whatever the morning brings, this cannot—will not—change. I am his and he is mine.

# Day Eight

*20<sup>th</sup> December*
*Park Place, New York City*

I t wasn't a dream. The warm, strong body beside me, the possessive arm wrapped around me holding me close. Last night and everything that transpired between Christian and I was real, not a dream.

Oh God.

Adrenalin pumps through my system as I realise what I've done. I've let him get too close, I've let him get inside my walls. This is not good, in fact this is a freaking disaster of bloody epic proportions. This is not going to end well.

The need to run seizes me and I begin to make my escape only to be thwarted by a large muscled arm.

'No you don't,' he says, his voice rough and scratchy and completely sexy with it's sleepiness.

'I—'

'No,' he says again, pulling me back against him.

I want to melt into him, I want to let go of all my worries, but my brain is engaged and scrambling, trying to find a way to rebuild the defences he broke through last night.

'Relax,' he whispers against my ear, his hot breath skittering over my skin and causing me to shiver with anticipation. His tongue traces the delicate shell of my ear and my eyes flutter shut as my body responds to him.

The fear and need to run dissipates under his ministrations. His hands caress me softly, barely making contact with my skin. His strong presence behind me, calms me. With him at my back, I know everything is going to be okay.

He trails soft kisses down my neck and I stretch my head to the side to give him more real estate to play with. He knows my body better than any other man in the past ever has. He knows my tells, reads my reactions and responds accordingly. Christian is a generous lover, making sure that I am just as invested in the experience as he is.

I roll towards him, needing his lips on mine, needing his demanding kiss to ground me, to reassure me. He doesn't disappoint me and I let him carry me away to that mystical place that we played in last night. He knows the way and leads me there, never faltering.

He seduces me with his hands and his mouth, lips and tongue. I crave his touch and he satisfies my increasing addiction to him. I know I am safe in his hands, I know that he will take me where I need to go and won't leave me unfulfilled and wanting. His touch is both new and familiar and I will never get enough of it.

I am undone by him, completely undone by the way he worships me. His hands are reverent and adoring, his kisses cherishing and endearing. I cannot hide from this man, he knows me, knows everything there is to know about me.

His lovemaking takes me higher until we crash together and break apart, our pieces transforming and reuniting themselves back together in a new way. We are eternally linked, the two of us, our souls fused together for eternity and the enormity of what we have built together is too much for me to contemplate.

'Good morning,' he rasps in my ear as we lay entwined, catching our breath.

'Good morning,' I whisper back.

'I'm not letting you go, Izzy,' he says, his arms tightening around me. 'So don't even try to run.'

I close my eyes, willing the tears not to fall. Who is this man that he can know me so intimately? Who am I in his arms?

'I've got you,' he whispers into my hair. 'I won't let you fall, Izzy.'

The problem, of course, is that I have already fallen. The life I knew, the life I have been living is smashed to pieces on the rocks below as I free fall off the cliff.

'I know there are things we need to work out. I know there are things we need to discuss, but you need to trust me.' His voice is steady and sure, and I cling to it. It is the only thing keeping me from bolting.

I close my eyes and breathe deeply, inhaling him; his strength, his scent, his essence. Although my brain is telling me to get as far away from him as possible, my heart convinces me to stay. I feel like I have been running for so long and I am weary. I want to stop running, to find rest and I know that Christian is the man to help me find it.

'I trust you,' I whisper, opening my eyes and searching his. 'Don't break my heart.'

He brushes a strand of hair from my forehead, his eyes concerned. 'I can't promise never to hurt you. But I can promise that I will never hurt you on purpose.'

It's enough. It's enough because I know that what he is saying is his absolute truth. We will hurt each other, it is inevitable, it is human nature. But I believe him when he says that he won't do anything intentionally to hurt me.

'I know,' I reply and I see the relief in his eyes.

He dips his head to brush his lips across mine. It's a seal, a promise. I relax against him letting his warmth, warm me.

'God, Izzy,' he says, breathing out harshly, 'The things you do to me.'

I snake my arms around him and hold him tight, telling him with my body that I feel the same, that I understand.

'You are an incredible woman,' he whispers against my temple. 'An amazing, wonderful, maddening woman.'

A bubble of laughter escapes my mouth as the tension from early is broken. I nuzzle his neck, nipping the soft skin with my teeth.

'You wouldn't have me any other way.'

His laughter rumbles in his chest and his arms tighten around me. 'You've got that right.'

My stomach takes that moment to remind me that I haven't eaten for a really long time.

'Hungry?' he asks as he rolls me on top of him. His eyes are dark with desire and I don't think it's food he's asking about.

WE EVENTUALLY MAKE it out of the bedroom and are currently sitting at the dining table demolishing a decadent feast of every conceivable breakfast food available. I don't think I've ever eaten so much in one sitting, but I am famished, and I'm not the only one. Christian has packed away a decent amount of food all on his own.

'Talk to me, Izzy,' he says.

'What do you want to know?' I ask, keeping it light, but still cautious.

'I know that your early experiences with Christmas were not ideal, but surely you've had better experiences since you've gown up?'

I shrug noncommittally.

'Tell me why you hate Christmas so much.'

I huff out a breath and stuff a piece of maple syrup drenched pancake in my mouth to give me time to come up with an answer. I chew slowly and then swallow, taking a sip of coffee before answering.

'I told you about my mother,' I begin. 'I told you about her ritual burning of our most precious things. Isn't that enough to turn anyone off Christmas?'

He watches me intently until I start to squirm under his gaze.

'I think there's more to it,' he says simply.

I shrug. 'Not really. It all comes back to that. When all of my friends were getting Barbie dolls and roller-skates and even horses sometimes, I had to choose between my favourite possessions and sacrifice them to a deity I didn't know or believe in. When I started getting gifts from friends, my mother would never let me keep them. One year she told me I had to break up with my high school boyfriend as a sacrifice.'

'Seriously? What did you do?'

'I lied to her. Told her I'd broken up with him and then kept seeing him behind her back.'

'Did she find out?'

I nod, remembering the fury that had transformed my usually calm mother into a screaming Banshee.

'I came home from school one day to find every possession I owned piled in the backyard and on fire. Her punishment for what she believed was my ultimate betrayal.'

'Holy shit,' he breathes. 'What did your father do?'

'Nothing,' I say, not looking at him. 'My father loved my mother to the point of obsession. He protected me when he could, but he would never outwardly defy her.'

He reaches over and covers my hand with his. 'I can't imagine growing up like that,' he says.

I look up at him and see pity in his eyes, the last thing I want him to feel for me. 'She wasn't always so... zealous. Most of the time she was a quintessential hippy-earth-mother type. It was only at Christmas that she became so fervent in her beliefs.'

'Still, it had to be hard on you.'

'Still is,' I say.

He raises an eyebrow at me. 'She still expects you to participate in her sacrifices? I thought she believed you find your own truth, your own religion.'

I huff out a laugh. 'No, that only applies to her. She believes in a matriarchal society, so until I choose a mate—her words—I am under her authority. She is the one who determines what our household believes, what we celebrate, what we mourn.'

'Geez,' he says with a shake of his head. 'You don't still live at home do you?'

'God no. I moved out as soon as I could and chose a university far enough away that she couldn't just 'pop' in to see me. I live in the city, several hours away from the home I grew up in.'

'But still you hate Christmas? Even though you know the difference now.'

'It's like exchanging one damaging tradition for another. I've seen how stressed out my friends get around the holidays. There's so much pressure to find the right gift and the financial strain is ridiculous. My friends spend time with people they don't even like, just because it's Christmas. They spend money they don't have on gifts for people they see once a year and even though it's touted to be the happiest time of the year, most of the people I socialise with are miserable. Do you know that the suicide rate is higher at Christmas time than at any other time of the year? I just can't get behind a day that is responsible for so much heartache.'

He looks at me with a strange look on his face, one I can't interpret.

'You know Christmas doesn't have to be either of those things, right? You've been exposed to the two extremes and neither one is what Christmas is really about.'

I shrug. 'So what's your Christmas story? Why do you love it so much.'

His eyes soften as he takes a moment to put into words what he wants to say.

'Christmas has always been a magical time for me. And before you say it's because I grew up in a wealthy family, I want you to know that my Christmases have very little to do with material things. It was the one time of the year when our family was all together and no business talk was allowed. My grandfather insisted on it, and although there is usually some grumbling for the first couple of days, by the time Christmas Day rolls around, everyone is having a good time, and it's easy to leave the business world behind.'

'That sounds idyllic,' I say. 'But not practical for everyone.'

He nods. 'True. But the point is we made the conscious choice to enjoy those days as a family and not just attend out of obligation. It's all about motivation and intention. We are a busy family, and for twelve days we come together and reconnect.'

'What about this year? Why aren't you with them now?'

His eyes shutter for a moment and I wonder if I've crossed some sort of invisible line, but then his expression clears and he answers.

'My grandfather died earlier this year,' he says softly.

'I'm sorry,' I say, reaching out to comfort him.

He smiles sadly at me. 'Thanks,' he says and then takes a breath.

'But what it means is that there are some things that I can't put off until after Christmas.'

'What about the rest of your family?'

'They are continuing the tradition,' he says. 'My uncle is now the patriarch, and my grandfather made him promise he wouldn't let the tradition die with him.'

'You miss them,' I say.

He nods, 'I do, but I will be with them on Christmas Day.'

'You're going home?'

'I am.'

'When?' my voice is more breathless than I would like but he is saved from answering by his phone.

THE MOMENT IS GONE. With the ringing of his cell phone, the real world broke through our bubble, and the haven we were existing in is shot to hell.

I stand from the table and begin to clean up the mess of our breakfast, letting him talk in privacy. I don't try to eavesdrop, as much as I want to. He walks out onto the balcony and I can see through the glass his furrowed brow and tight jaw. The easy, relaxed man that I had been having breakfast with is gone and the man that stands out there on the balcony is the businessman Christian, a man I don't know the first thing about.

Maybe it is time to Google him.

I try to hold on to the shredded pieces of our morning, but they disappear like smoke. We had pressed pause on life for a little while, but it is time to get back to reality. Even as I try to believe that what Christian and I have enjoyed over the last twelve hours is something that can last, I can feel it slipping away.

I watch as he disconnects from the call and runs an agitated hand through his hair. The tension is clear in the way he holds his body and I have a premonition of dread. Whoever was on the other end of that phone call is about to destroy the fragile connection that Christian and I have begun to build.

I pretend not to notice as I go about clearing the table. He walks back into the room, and I can see the sadness in his eyes. Our pleasant interlude has come to an end, and I can tell that he also knows there is heartache to come.

With determination he walks over to me and threads his fingers through my hair, cupping my jaw in his large hands. He stares into my eyes before lowering his head and kissing me deeply. I'm frightened now, frightened by his desperation as he kisses me like his life depends on it.

'Izzy,' he breathes when he lifts his head, pulling me into his chest and rubbing his cheek on my hair. 'I want you to know, that whatever happens next, I never meant to hurt you.'

I try to pull away, I need to see his eyes, but he holds me tightly, breathing me in.

And then he is gone.

I stand there stunned by what just happened. What does he mean when he says he never meant to hurt me? I am so confused. It was only an hour ago he was promising me that he would have my back, that he was reassuring me that what was between us was real and not just a dream. Now he is gone and I am left floundering.

What an arsehole!

Anger is my default. Whenever I feel insecure or unsure or displaced, anger is my saviour. I welcome it, I welcome the familiar feelings of rage. It gives me strength, it makes me feel strong.

I am angry at him, furious, in fact. How dare he turn my world upside-down and then just leave. Who does that? Who just walks out after an incredible night of sex? Who walks away when they have prised open the very heart of another person and leaves them to clean up the devastation left behind?

I feel like throwing something or punching something. I want to wreak havoc, a one woman tornado destroying everything in my path. I curl my fingers into fists, willing myself not to start throwing the dishes off the room service cart. The need to hear the satisfying tinkle of smashed crockery almost overrides my common sense. I breathe through it, maintaining my calm, calling on every single anger management technique I can remember to stop myself from losing my shit.

Ah, what the hell.

As the first plate hits the tiled floor, a little bit of my sanity is restored. A cup, a glass, a large platter—each one makes a distinct sound and combines in a symphony that soothes me. I'm not throwing them, just dropping them onto the floor in front of me, watching them break apart just as my heart is breaking. Before I know it, I am gleefully destroying every single plate, saucer, bowl and cup until I am breathing hard and feeling the euphoria left behind by my reckless and insane act.

Did I mention that I have an anger management issue?

I look at the destruction I have wrought. It seems fitting that the mess on the floor resembles the destruction inside me. See, this is why I can't have nice things. They always get destroyed. I should've known better than to let him get so close to me. I should've known better than to open my heart.

What's done is done. The breaking of dishes has been cathartic and now I need to get on with the business of rebuilding my destroyed life. How can one man make such a mess in such a short amount of time? I have been so careful for so long that I didn't think it was possible for anyone to burrow so completely into my life. But I can't change it, I can only move on.

It is a lesson, one that I need to learn from. Maybe this is the Goddess's revenge on me for all the years I have refused to sacrifice to her, except that I don't believe in her. She is my mother's truth, not mine. Regardless, it is a lesson, whether from the universe or some form of deity, and I need to learn this lesson, as hard as it might be.

If only I hadn't let myself care so much, if only I had held back a little of my heart instead of handing it all to him on a platter. If I had just kept a little distance between us, if I hadn't let him consume me so completely, maybe we could have had something for a little bit longer. But that wasn't how things in my life usually went. Everything I've ever loved has been taken away from me, why should this be any different?

## Day Nine

*21<sup>st</sup> December*
*Park Place, New York City*

He didn't call. I hadn't really expected him to, but a small part of my heart foolishly hoped.

I spent the rest of the day holed up in the bedroom of my suite. The maid grumbled about the broken dishes as she cleaned up the mess, but I didn't offer an explanation or apology. I made a nest in the bed, alternatively breathing in the scent he'd left on the pillow and throwing it across the room because I couldn't stand the smell.

Not yet ready to wash his touch off my body, not yet willing to remove that last link between us, I refused to shower. I ordered room service and made them leave it at the door so I wouldn't have to endure the pitying looks. I watched sappy movies and angry, violent action movies with lots of explosions and fight scenes. I cried, big heart wrenching sobs and screamed angry curses until I had finally fallen into a fitful sleep.

I don't do breakups well, obviously.

When I open my eyes this morning, they are sore and crusty, and I imagine I look like I've been on a weekend bender. I don't care. In fact, I

80

don't care about anything. I've entered the numb stage. My head feels like it is stuffed full of cotton wool, and my hearing is dull, like sounds are coming to me from underwater.

I crawl out of bed and strip the sheets robotically, dumping them outside the door of my suite. I shower without thought, dressing without intention. I'm drifting. Part of my brain is telling me I'm being an idiot, and that strong, independent women don't let men affect their lives like this, but I don't listen to it. I know I will survive, that I will go on, but right now, I just need to let myself heal however it needs to.

I open my laptop listlessly and do some more half-arsed research for my article, but it is a waste of time and I know it. There is nothing I can learn from the World Wide Web, and at this stage, it looks like my article is just going to be the same regurgitated facts that every other Mr Toys article has spouted. I know nothing new. I haven't discovered who the mysterious Mr Toys is, and it is going to be a black mark against my reputation.

I don't care.

My phone rings, and I answer automatically.

'Isobel, please tell me you have something, anything.'

Maryanne sounds frantic, which is not at all like her.

'I'm sorry, Maryanne, I have nothing.'

'Goddamn it!'

'Whoa, settle down. I can still write the article, there just won't be anything spectacular about it. The guy must have some iron-clad non-disclosure agreements with his staff to have gone this long with no one spilling the beans.'

'You don't understand,' Maryanne says tiredly. 'We need this story. The magazine is on the line.'

Her comment pierces my fugue. 'What do you mean, "the magazine is on the line"?'

'Just that. We are losing advertisers, and our parent company is threatening to shut us down.'

'What!' I jump to my feet, my heartbreak overridden for the moment by the possible loss of my career, a career I have poured my entire soul into for the last six years.

'You know that old man Hayden died earlier this year.'

'Yeah, so? What does that have to do with us?'

'We are owned by the Hayden Group, and the old man has been replaced by his grandson.'

'Okay,' I say, still not understanding how this affects my livelihood.

'He's cleaning house,' she says simply. 'Every company and subsidiary has come under the microscope. Remember a couple of weeks ago when all those people lost their jobs?'

'The Hayden Bros. Department store staff?'

'Yeah, them. That was because of wonder boy.'

'Bloody hell.'

'Exactly. He's certainly making a big splash and fast becoming the most hated man in Australia.'

'Shit, shit, shit,' I say, beginning to pace.

'So you see why I need that article. If you can pull it off, I'm positive we can stave off the axe. It will be our biggest issue yet. He is holding a press conference in an hour to announce the next round of cuts. We need you to get that story, Isobel. We are all depending on you.'

I disconnect from Maryanne and sit in a daze. My entire world is falling down around me. First Christian destroys my personal life, and now some nameless Richie Rich with a trust fund and something to prove is trying to destroy my professional life. It's the motivation I need to get off my arse and do something rather than wallowing in my self-pity.

I walk over to the living area and flick on the television with the remote. I sit on the couch and surf through the channels until I see the Hayden Group logo behind an empty podium. The scrolling ticker tape at the bottom of the screen informs me that the press conference is live from New York City, and I wonder if I have enough time to get down there before it starts. I have my press credentials, so I shouldn't have any trouble getting in; I just don't know where they are.

A suited man walks onto the screen, adjusting the podium and placing a glass of water on the small table beside it. I know that man. I've seen him in the lobby. The press conference is being held at the hotel.

I scramble to my feet and grab my handbag, double-checking that I have my credentials. I run out of the room, and punch the elevator call button impatiently. Finally the elevator arrives, and I step in, checking the buttons for the conference room. I press the button and then chew my thumbnail nervously as the elevator descends. The doors open and I rush out, heading for the crowd of reporters walking into the conference room. I flash my badge and barge my way through, grabbing a seat towards the front.

THERE IS an anticipatory atmosphere as the journalists fill the room. We are like sharks, scenting blood in the water. We all want a piece of the man that the Australian press has branded The Executioner. There have even been cartoons drawn in his honour showing him wielding a large executioner's axe as he indiscriminately destroys people's lives.

How did I not know that this man was ultimately my boss? A faux pas on my part. I have always been more interested in my immediate circle of influence, forgetting that Iconoclast was part of a conglomerate that had shareholders to please. We had been pretty much left to our own devices without pressure from above to publish more crowd-pleasing articles. That was until now. Now we had been called to task and made to prove ourselves, and I was the one letting the team down.

Christian had derailed me, the first man to have ever managed it. My career has always come first, and I have left dates hanging without so much as a phone call in order to chase a story. But Christian had completely thrown me off my game within days of meeting me only to leave me swinging in the breeze with my pink polka dot undies hanging out for all to see.

This is why I didn't let myself fall in love. Love was dangerous. Love led to bad things happening. Case in point.

God, I was an idiot. I thought I knew better; I thought I was stronger.

Well, I'd learned my lesson, and I wouldn't be letting my guard down anytime soon. I could be thankful to Christian for that at the very least. He had cured me of that deadly affliction called love.

I notice a change in the atmosphere as the journalists around me lean forward, ready to feast on the man about to make an announcement that could very possibly devastate my life.

He is tall, his blonde head showing above the other heads surrounding him. His shoulders are broad, and he wears his suit as if it were a well-worn t-shirt. I can't see his face, but I know. I know who he is, and I want to throw up. The man who holds my career in his hands is the same man who, all too recently, smashed my heart to bits.

Oh shit.

And then I realise why he has always felt familiar to me, why I had recognised his face that first time in the airport, why his name had sounded familiar. The pieces click together, and I want to slap myself. I have been sleeping with the enemy. Christian Palmer is the most hated man in Australia.

How could I not have known that the man I was cavorting with was, ostensibly, my boss? But he'd known, from that second day when he'd rescued me and brought me to the hotel, he'd known I worked for Iconoclast. And he hadn't told me.

His cryptic last words to me yesterday now made more sense. He knew what was coming; he knew I was going to lose my job; he knew he was about to blow up my entire life.

And. He. Walked. Away.

It was like a knife to the chest to realise that everything I had worked so hard for was about to be destroyed by the only man I have ever fallen in love with.

'Good afternoon,' he says, and I have to close my eyes against the pain his voice creates. 'Thank you for coming this afternoon. If you could all please hold your questions until the end, I will answer as many as I can.' He clears his throat and takes a sip of water. He doesn't look nervous. He looks authoritative and in control. 'I called this press conference today to inform the public of our decision to close the publishing arm of the Hayden Group. This will affect many publications, including newspapers and magazines. We did not arrive at this decision lightly. The board discussed this decision well into the night and it was finally decided early this morning by a closely contested vote. The next few months will be spent winding up the individual operations, and many of the existing staff will be absorbed into other areas of The Hayden Group. The publications affected are: Morning News Daily, Finance and Investment Review, Tomorrow's Inventions Today,

Today's Woman, Celebs, and Iconoclast.' He looks right at me when he names my magazine, and his eyes are shuttered and cold. It would have been kinder for him to stab me with an ice pick. 'Questions?'

I tune out the press pack as they lob pointless questions at him. None of it matters. My job is defunct. There is no way I can be assimilated into his organisation. I'm a reporter, and he no longer has a company that needs a reporter.

I wonder what will happen to the rest of the people I work with. Maryanne will probably be offered early retirement, but even if she isn't, she will bounce back. The woman is a legend and a really talented editor. A couple of the other older guys would more than likely take their redundancies and retire happily. The office staff would surely be reassigned to other parts of the Hayden Group, which left me and maybe two other reporters with no prospects.

I had burnt bridges before coming to Iconoclast. I hated that other editors watered down my articles, making them less inflammatory to keep the big bosses happy. I probably wouldn't be able to get another job in the Australian press. Iconoclast and Maryanne had been my last resort. I was good at what I did, but I was awful at pandering to those in authority. It would take a miracle for me to find another publication willing to take a chance on me. I was washed up at the grand old age of twenty-seven.

'Isobel.'

I look up into those eyes that I had so loved and felt sick. He had betrayed me in the worst way, and now I had nothing.

'You knew,' I say, standing, not caring about the straggling journalists who hadn't yet left. 'You've known all this time, and you said nothing.'

Christian sighed and pinched the bridge of his nose. 'No,' he said resignedly, 'I didn't know.'

'But you knew you were my boss, and you knew my job was on the chopping block.' My voice had risen, and we had attracted attention.

'Come with me,' he says, taking me by the elbow and leading me to a small room that had served as a green room before the press conference.

He lets go of me and closes the door, taking the time to lock it. I wait while he gathers himself together before facing me. When he turns around, I see the devastation in his eyes, and my armour cracks a little.

'That's why you left yesterday, isn't it?' I ask, determined to keep it together, to keep my anger stoked and blazing.

'Yes,' he says. 'An emergency board meeting had been called to discuss our options.'

'And I was the sacrifice.'

His eyes flare and his mouth drops open. 'No,' he says, walking towards me, arms outstretched. He stops before we actually make contact, and my body yearns to feel his arms around me. 'I tried to save Iconoclast. I wasn't lying when I said it was my favourite magazine. It was also my grandfather's favourite. It was his brainchild.'

'Well you didn't try hard enough!' I snap like a tempestuous child. 'You have effectively ruined my career. No one else will employ me, Christian.'

He rakes his hand through his hair and grits his teeth. 'What would you have me do, Isobel? Save your job just because we slept together? What makes your job any more important than the hundreds of other people I would have had to fire to keep your magazine alive?'

'What the hell are you talking about?'

'Iconoclast has never once turned a profit the entire time it has been in circulation. It costs me more money every year, and now with the loss of yet another advertiser, we just couldn't justify the cost. By closing down the publishing arm of the Hayden Group, it means I can keep paying the wages of hundreds of other employees, people with families, people who are only a year or two away from retirement. I'm sorry you are losing your job, but it is the lesser of two evils.'

I don't know what to say to that. He's right, of course. How could he keep the magazine going when it wasn't paying its way? It doesn't make it hurt any less, though.

He exhales harshly and paces away from me. I can see how hard this is for him. I can see the stress and tension tightening his body into knots.

'You could have warned me,' I say.

He stops and turns to face me. 'I couldn't,' he says, pleading with me to understand with his eyes. 'You are a member of the press, and I couldn't leak what was happening before the decision had been made.'

'You didn't trust me,' I say.

'You followed me,' he retorts. 'You followed me instead of just coming out and asking me. I didn't know what you would do with the information if I gave it to you.'

'So that's it then,' I say. 'That's all there is for us.'

'No, Isobel, no.' He grasps my upper arms and pulls me close. I want to melt into him. I want to give in to my body, but I can't. I can't let him take from me the small amount of self-respect that I've rebuilt.

'Yes, Christian. What happened between us... it was a mistake.' I wrench myself away from him and head for the door.

'Please, Isobel, don't do this. We can work this out, please.'

I swing around to face him. 'No, Christian, we can't. We are from two different worlds. We live two different lives. This could never work between us.'

'You're not even giving us a chance,' he says. 'You're walking away at the first setback.'

'No, I'm just seeing the truth about us.'

'What you're seeing is a lie. A lie your mother perpetuated with her ridiculous sacrifices. You're afraid, Isobel, afraid of getting too close to me. Can't you see? Your mother taught you that whatever you love will be taken away from you, and so now you won't let yourself love. You're afraid of it being taken away from you, so you have created these walls around your life to protect yourself. I understand, but I'm trying to show you that your mother is wrong. What she did was wrong. It's okay to love. It's okay to love me!'

He is breathing heavily, and I see the desperation in his eyes. I know that what he is saying is true. I know I am afraid to love, afraid to lose, but hasn't it just been proven to me yet again? I love my job, and it is being ripped from me. I love Christian, and I have to give him up too.

I walk towards him and reach out to brush his cheek with my hand. I see the hope in his eyes, and I smile sadly.

'What we shared the other night,' I begin and then swallow back tears. 'It was the most amazing night of my life.' I reach up and brush my lips softly against his. 'I will never forget you or our night together.'

I turn and walk away.

'Izzy,' he pleads, and I stop with my hand on the door.

'Goodbye, Christian.'

# Day Ten

*22nd December*
*Park Place, New York City*

I 'm not proud of the amount of alcohol I imbibed last night, and I'm definitely paying the price for it now. After the press conference, I came back here and drowned my sorrows with the help of the ridiculously overpriced mini-bar. I had cried myself out, but there was still mourning to do. I think I hit every stage—multiple times—last night, but I kept coming back to anger. I didn't break any more dishes, but I had contemplated pulling a rockstar move and heaving the television out the window, only there wasn't a pool anywhere below my window and I would probably kill some unsuspecting pedestrian. Christian was not worth going to jail for.

I slept fitfully, waking up several times during the night, one of which was to empty my stomach of the unholy mix of drinks I had swallowed. Luckily, I made it to the bathroom and didn't have a mess to clean up this morning.

Right now, I sit on the balcony looking listlessly out at the park view and wondering what the hell I am going to do with the rest of my life. Thankfully, the suite has a handy-dandy Keurig, and I brewed myself a surprisingly decent cup of coffee, which was helping to calm my roiling stomach and jump-start my misfiring brain.

My phone sits on the table beside my laptop, but I turned the thing off when I got back to the hotel yesterday and refuse to turn it back on. Maryanne would no doubt have been blowing it up with calls and messages, and I really couldn't face her disappointment right now. My laptop had pinged a couple of times with incoming emails, but they were easy to ignore. I really didn't want to have any contact with the outside world before I had found some sort of equilibrium within myself.

A knock at my door pulled me out of my musings, so I get to my feet and shuffled inside. I opened the door to see a familiar bellboy holding a gift-wrapped box.

'Ms Carmichael,' he says in greeting. 'This came for you.' He hands me the box, and I look at it curiously, hoping for a card or something to identify the sender. 'I think it's an invitation,' he whispered conspiratorially to me.

I raised an eyebrow skeptically. 'An invitation?'

'To the Mr Toys Extravaganza,' he explained.

That made my eyes widen in surprise. 'How do you know?'

He shrugs sheepishly. 'I've seen one or two of them before,' he says.

I smile brightly at him. 'Thanks for the heads up,' I say.

He looks like he wants to say something else, and I stand there waiting him out.

His cheeks flush before he speaks. 'I hope you don't find this out of line, but after our talk the other day I thought you might be interested in this.' He digs into his uniform pocket and pulls out a photograph, handing it over to me. 'This was the Christmas Day when the group home I was in received the gifts from Mr Toys.'

I look down at the picture and see a group of very happy-looking teens flanked by a couple of older men and women. One man in particular grabs my attention. He is quite a bit older than the rest, and he is dressed in a suit. But what gets my attention are the sparkling blue eyes that look directly into the camera and a very familiar smile.

'Who's this?' I ask, pointing to the man in question.

'Charlie,' he says, 'Charlie Hayden. He was a sponsor of the home.'

The bellboy's face softened as he looked down at the man. 'He would visit us whenever he was in the country, and he loved to just sit with us and talk. I had no grandparents, but I like to think that if I did, they would've been like him.'

I hand the photo back to him, and he tucks it away in his pocket.

'Thanks for sharing that with me. It seems like it was a really happy time for you.'

He beams a smile at me. 'It really was. I'm so grateful to Charlie and to all the others in that home. I know other kids who weren't so lucky, and I'm just glad I didn't end up like some of them.'

He gives me a wave and refuses my attempt to give him a tip, and I watch him retreat down the corridor. I close the door thoughtfully and wander back into the suite, mulling over the photograph and Charlie Hayden. His eyes and his smile were so much like Christian's that they had to be related. Was Charlie Hayden Christian's grandfather?

I sit the box on the table and walk back out to the balcony, waking up my laptop with the press of a key. I bring up Google and type in 'Charlie Hayden' and sit back as the search page populates with thousands of responses. Clicking on a news item, I see it is the article that covered his funeral. The reporter practically gushes with praise for the man and his many and varied philanthropic endeavours. There is a photo of the family and I catch my breath as I see Christian, his eyes a picture of misery as he carries the coffin of his grandfather.

An email notification pops up in the corner of my screen, and I am surprised to see who it is from. Grace Hayden. Surely it couldn't be any relation to Charlie Hayden? That would be just too weird. I click open the notification and cannot believe what I read. Grace Hayden is the late Charlie's wife, and she'd like to talk to me about possibly writing her husband's memoirs. It is an intriguing offer, but a hint of suspicion snakes its way into my brain. Was this Christian's doing?

AGAINST MY BETTER JUDGEMENT, and completely because of my innate curiosity, I agree to meet Grace Hayden. The idea of writing a biography of one of the most loved Australian business people is worming its way into my brain, and I'm already itching to get going on the research. I've never considered writing a book before, but this suggestion has me feeling a spark of excitement that I thought I'd never feel again.

I dress with care and take extra time doing my hair and makeup. Grace Hayden is an Australian icon, and I know I'll need to make a good impression on her if she is going to consider giving me access to her husband's private life.

I love finding out the real story behind the public faces of the people I interview. There is so much you can learn about their motivations and their decision-making processes when you have a little bit of insight into what goes on behind closed doors. If I accept this offer, if I even get an offer, I will insist on absolute access, with nothing off limits. It's the only way I know how to work.

She sends a car for me, and I fidget nervously as it glides through the city and out towards the Hayden estate. It's an hour and a half out of the city, and I try to keep myself distracted by gazing out at the passing scenery. I am surprised at the understated area where the estate is located. I expected a row of grand mansions, but they look more like homesteads. The limousine turns down a narrow road, and I see the large home beyond the tall brick and wrought-iron gates.

A chauffeur opens the door for me, and I look around appreciatively. There is a comforting atmosphere, almost a feeling of coming home, and I shake off the unfamiliar feeling. This is a job, or could be a job, and I have to be on my game.

I take the stairs, and the front door opens before I reach it. I am ushered into the high-ceilinged foyer and directed into a comfy sitting room. An older woman, whom I recognise from my internet searches, stands to greet me with a smile. She walks towards me, hands outstretched, and takes mine in hers like we're old friends.

'Thank you, Ms Carmichael, for coming.'

'It's my pleasure, Mrs Hayden,' I say. 'You have a lovely home.'

She looks around the room, and her face softens. 'I enjoy the time I spend here, but it's not quite the same without my Charlie.'

I give her a moment, surprised by the wash of emotions that crosses her face. She must have really loved her husband, a fact I find surprising.

It's very rare, in my experience, to find a couple with as much money and influence as this couple has, that are genuinely in love.

'Come, sit,' she says, turning from me and indicating the overstuffed sofas that look like the most comfortable things I've ever seen. 'Would you like tea or maybe a cold drink?'

'Tea would be lovely,' I say, perching on one of the sofas, knowing that if I sit back I may never get up again.

We make small talk as she settles herself, and once the tea is served, with what looks suspiciously like homemade scones with fresh jam and cream, I take a breath and speak.

'Mrs Hayden,' I begin, and she waves me off.

'Please call me Grace.'

'Grace,' I begin again, 'I was very intrigued to receive your invitation, but also a little suspicious. Christian didn't put you up to this, did he?'

Her look of genuine surprise answers my question. 'Christian? Do you know Christian?'

I breathe a sigh of relief. I don't think I could have accepted the job if I had known Christian had set it up. 'I met him earlier this week, and the timing of your request piqued my curiosity.'

She frowns. 'I don't quite understand, dear.'

'The Hayden Group announced yesterday that they were closing the publishing arm of the company, effectively putting me out of a job.'

'Oh,' she says, 'I had no idea.'

'So why did you contact me?'

'Charlie loved your articles so much,' she says, her face going soft again. 'I would often hear him chortling to himself over something you'd written and declaring what a spitfire you must be. He often commented to me he wished he could meet you, to sit down and have a conversation with you.'

I can't help the blush that stains my cheeks at the praise. Mostly I got raked over the coals for my articles, and I was no doubt more than responsible for the magazine losing advertisers. I was inordinately pleased that someone enjoyed reading my work.

I settled back on the sofa and pulled out my tablet, opening it to the note-taking app. I set my phone on the coffee table and pressed record on the voice memo app. 'You don't mind if I record this interview, do you?' I ask.

'Not at all,' Grace replies. 'Does this mean you'll do it? You'll write Charlie's biography?'

'I would love to write your husband's biography,' I say honestly. I don't know what it is about this family, but they seem to have a way of getting under my skin. 'Why don't you start with how you met.'

Listening to Grace talk about her husband makes me feel a little sad for what I may have given up with Christian. Here is a woman who had been married to the same man for over forty years, and she had loved him until the day he died. Was it really possible to have such a relationship with another person? My only role models had been my parents or friends' parents. My own family was more dysfunctional than I cared to admit, and I'm pretty sure my father's love for my mother bordered on obsession and was not at all healthy. The parents of my friends hadn't been the ideal picture of wedded bliss, with more than half of them separating and eventually divorcing. But listening to Grace speak, I feel a small spark of hope that there is a chance for me, a very remote chance, but still a chance.

I CLOSE the suite door behind me and lean against it, thinking back over the two hours I spent with Grace Hayden. What an amazing woman and what an amazing family. It is a credit to her and her husband that they have raised such a well-balanced family with the pressures of not just running a multimillion-dollar business, but also growing it to the massive conglomerate it is today.

They'd started with one department store on Sydney's Oxford Street. It had in fact been Charlie's grandfather's store. Jack Hayden and his brother had started the store towards the end of the 1800s, around 1885 or so. By the time Charlie was born, the company was going through hard times. Two World Wars and the Great Depression hit them hard. Charlie had convinced his father to stick with it, and he managed to completely revamp the store and make it a mecca for the *nouveau riche* that flooded the city. Grace had gotten a job at Hayden

Bros. when they opened their new store on Pitt Street, Sydney's elite shopping high street. She and Charlie met on the job, and he pursued her with single-mindedness until she agreed to go out with him. It had been a whirlwind romance, and they were married six weeks later.

Over the years, I have heard varying reports on Charlie Hayden, but most of the negative press had come from his competitors, and there had never been even one disgruntled employee selling a salacious story to the media. Even now, with the cutbacks that Christian had been instigating, it wasn't the employees who were leading the posse demanding Christian's head; it was the media sensationalising the situation. The fact that he'd made the announcements so close to Christmas had done nothing to garner him favour in the press and in the most recent articles I had read, they were saying his grandfather would be turning in his grave if he could see what his grandson was doing.

An unfair criticism and one I know would be causing Christian heartache. In the short time I had known him, I had seen Christian's affection for his grandfather, and I know that he is currently in a tough position. Which made the way I treated him the other day and the hurtful things I said to him unforgivable. I had reacted out of fear and hurt and lashed out at the one man who had been nothing but wonderful to me.

The unopened gift box on the table catches my eye. I have been so caught up in the whole Charlie Hayden thing that I had completely forgotten about it. I walk slowly towards it, wondering how on earth this made up an invitation? Untying the red bow, I lift the lid on the box, only to find a colourfully decorated box inside. The new box has a small arm protruding from the side. I sit the box on the table and turn the handle. Tinny jack-in-the-box music plays, and then the top pops open, and a jack-in-the-box jumps out, startling a joyful laugh out of me.

Thankfully, it's not one of those creepy jack-in-the-boxes with their freaky clown faces. This one is cute, and in his hand is a card with my name on it and a time, date and address. It is indeed an invitation to the Mr Toys Extravaganza, and I can't help but wonder just how I lucked out to get this invite. The only person I can imagine who would have the pull to organise an invitation for me was Christian.

After spending the day with his grandmother, my feelings towards him changed. She showed me family photos, and little Christian was just as cute as grown-up Christian, and those sparkling blue eyes still had the same effect on me. The man is my kryptonite, but I was starting to feel like that wasn't such a bad thing. There were worse ways to die than in the arms of a gorgeous billionaire with a killer smile.

I should call him. I should thank him for the invitation, but I'm scared. It's hard for me to admit to being scared. I'm the fearless journalist who has faced the wrath of more than one irate man after accusing him of something he had thought well hidden. Nothing scares me, except maybe the thought that Christian no longer wants anything to do with me.

He wouldn't have sent the invitation to me if he never wanted to see me again, would he? What if I rang him and he tells me he wasn't the one who sent the invitation? What if there is the same frigid ice in his voice that I heard at the press conference? I don't think my heart could take it.

I pick up my phone and scroll through the missed calls. There are a ton from Maryanne, but there are also quite a few from Christian. Surely he wouldn't have called so many times just to yell at me? I hit the button for my voice messages and listen as his voice comes through the speaker, causing a full body shiver.

*'Isobel, call me, please. I don't want to leave it like this.'*

*'Still not talking to me? Please just call me.'*

*'Izzy, this is ridiculous. Call me.'*

*'Come on Izzy, don't shut me out. Call me back, I'm worried about you.'*

*'Call me.'*

*'Please call me.'*

*'Izzy.'*

*'Okay, fine. It's two a.m. and I can't sleep because I'm worried about you. I understand that you're angry and hurt and afraid, but this is not the end for us, Isobel. You may think you can run from me and hurl all the insults you like at me, but I am not giving up on you. This thing between us is real, and I am going to do everything in my power to make sure you know exactly how I feel about you. The very last thing I want is for my first*

*time telling you I love you to be over the phone, but since you stubbornly refuse to call me back, here it is. I love you, Isobel, and I know you love me too. You are not running away from this. I won't let you. Call me, dammit!'*

My knees turn to jelly and I sink into the nearest chair as I replay that last message. Christian is in love with me. My cheeks are wet as I hear the words again. I hit redial and listen to his phone ring out. I hear his greeting on his voice mail and sob as the beep sounds.

'I love you too,' I whisper before hanging up.

# Day Eleven

*23rd December*
*Park Place, New York City*

For the first time in days, I wake up feeling refreshed and ready to face the day. I order a light breakfast from room service and set myself up at the dining room table with my laptop and notes from yesterday's interview with Grace. I am so inspired that the words flow from my fingertips as I write the love story of Grace and Charlie, my face smiling as I imagine how he must have bugged her until she finally relented and agreed to a date.

The more I write, the more I see how much alike Charlie and Christian are. Their similarity in looks is just the tip of the iceberg. Christian is almost a mini-me of Charlie, and my heart fills for the man I have fallen in love with. I wish I could have met his grandfather. I wish I could have met the man who'd had such a profound impact on Christian. I'd like to shake his hand.

There is a knock on the suite door, and I get up to let in the room service attendant. My favourite bellboy follows him in, and his eyes are alight with mischief.

'These are for you,' he says with a wink, handing me a large garment bag and a shopping bag.

I tip them both and then unzip the garment bag in excitement. Inside is a gorgeous black velvet gown. I run my fingers over the soft pile of the fabric and hold it up to take in the full effect. It's a long, slim sheath with a long slit in the side that will no doubt reach mid-thigh. Sparkling crystals glint against the dark fabric, clustering around the hem and petering out the higher up the skirt they go. It has a simple scoop neckline, and a sheer chiffon cape falls from the shoulders. The back of the dress...well, there is no back, which means there will be no bra either.

I lay the dress reverently on the bed and look inside the shopping bag. There is a Louboutin box nestled among the tissue paper. Inside are a pair of black stilettos with the signature red soles. I have coveted a pair of Louboutin for as long as I can remember, but have never had enough money to buy them. Holding these in my hands is like holding the Hope Diamond.

I sneak another look in the bag and discover a thick, creamy envelope with my name scrawled across the front. Careful not to tear it, I pull out a card with an appointment and an address on it. A free spa day! I crush the card to my chest and do a little spin. There is no signature to reveal who it is from, but I know. This is all from Christian.

I shower and dress, scoffing down my breakfast in order to be on time for my appointment and head out the door. A car is waiting for me and it whisks me away to an exclusive spa centre. I have never been so pampered in my life and I am so relaxed that the waxing treatment doesn't even send me screaming from the room.

When I'm sufficiently plucked and pummelled, I'm taken into the salon where my hair is highlighted and trimmed before being styled in a messy, yet classy, up-do. My makeup is done, giving my skin a flawless appearance, and then I'm sent back into the car and driven back to the hotel. The kitchen sends up a light supper for me, which I eat with relish, and then I take my time dressing. I wear my sexiest knickers and thigh-high stockings with a thick lace garter at the top. The dress fits me like a glove, and the shoes feel like slippers as I slide them on. I look in the mirror and can't believe that the woman looking back is me. I have never looked this good.

This all feels like a fairytale, and the cautious part of me keeps whispering not to get my hopes up. The part of me that has protected me from heartache my entire life, counsels caution and not to get in too deep. But I'm sick of listening to that part of me. I'm sick of missing out on the rollercoaster of life because I have to keep my heart locked up tight. I moved out of home to get away from my mother's destructive influence only to realise that I had taken it with me. The voice in my head is my mother's, and she is still trying to ruin my life.

I take a deep breath and close my eyes, imagining Christian's smile, his sparkling blue eyes, the way his lips feel when he kisses me. I think about how different a person I am when I'm around him. He brings out the best in me and I like that woman, I want to be her all the time. Christian is good for me, and he makes me feel good too. I would be an absolute idiot to walk away from him because of some twisted ritual my mother believes in.

Opening my eyes, I look myself over one more time and I smile. It's time to take back my man and, make no mistake, he is mine. Christian Palmer will not know what hit him.

THE SHROUD COVERING Toyland has been removed, and the front of the store is lit up with searchlights and coloured fairy lights. The large toy soldiers that had stood sentinel along the front of the store now stand in formation on either side of a red carpet that leads up to the front doors. There are acrobats and performers on stilts, clowns and ballerinas entertaining the crowd as my limousine pulls up. The door is opened, and I am handed out by a smiling attendant. I walk up the red carpet, mesmerised by the spectacle going on around me. Fire dancers stop for me a moment as I watch them perform.

A warm arm slips around my waist, and I feel a hard chest behind me. My eyes flutter shut as I breathe in his familiar cinnamon and spice scent.

'You came,' he whispers in my ear before placing a soft kiss on my neck.

A full body shiver courses through me and I lean back against him, soaking up his strength. 'How could I stay away?' I say.

He turns me in his arms and gazes down at me, searching my eyes. I press up onto my toes and brush my lips across his.

'I'm sorry,' I murmur against his mouth. 'I'm sorry for letting my fear get the better of me.'

His arms tighten around me and he kisses me softly before holding my head against his chest. I can hear his heartbeat pounding under his white shirt and I know mine is pounding just as hard.

'Come on,' he says huskily. 'Let's go inside.'

The inside of the toy store is a wonderland. It is full of every toy that a kid could dream of and a lot of the adults currently milling around are having the time of their lives reliving their childhood.

'It's amazing,' I say, turning to Christian.

He smiles with pride and then looks down at me with an expression that can only be described as adoration.

'Not as amazing as you,' he says.

'Isobel!'

Christian looks up puzzled as his grandmother joins us. I accept her hug and exchange a kiss on the cheek with her as Christian watches on, nonplussed.

'Grace. It's so lovely to see you again.'

'You know my grandmother?' Christian asks after he greets Grace with a kiss.

'We met yesterday,' she explains.

I nod. 'Your grandmother has asked me to write your grandfather's biography.'

His eyes widen in surprise and I'm suddenly afraid that he won't approve. What if he doesn't want me snooping through his family's past?

'That's wonderful,' he says, looking between the two of us, trying to understand.

Grace pats his arm comfortingly. 'Your grandfather always spoke so highly of her writing and I thought he would approve if she was the one to write his story.'

'What I've heard so far is fascinating,' I say. 'And I've already started putting some of my thoughts down on paper.'

'We will get together in the New Year and I will give you access to his personal effects so you can get a better read on him.'

Christian looks alarmed at this news. 'You'll give her grandfather's journals?' he asks.

'Of course,' Grace says, unperturbed. 'She can't very well write his biography without them.'

'What about—'

'Oh, hush, sweetheart. We'll talk about it later.' She turns back to me. 'Are you staying through Christmas?'

'I'm scheduled to fly back to Australia Christmas morning.'

'Oh no,' she says with a shake of her head. 'You should change that. I'd love you to join the family for Christmas. You are going to be spending so much time with us over the next however many months, you may as well meet them all in one fell swoop.'

'You're having Christmas here?' I ask, looking at Christian. 'I assumed that you would be flying home—'

'Seeing as though Christian has broken with tradition this year to work,' she threw him a stern glance. 'The family has flown out here instead.'

Christian blushed. 'I was going to tell you, but—'

'It's okay. I know that the last few days have been kind of... hectic.'

He gives me a soft smile. 'So will you come? Will you celebrate Christmas with us?'

I look between the two of them and see genuine eagerness in their eyes. Maybe it's time I start making new Christmas traditions instead of being so driven by the ones I grew up with.

'I'd love too,' I say.

'Excellent,' Grace says with a clap of her hands. 'Now, I need to socialise.'

She turns and walks into the fray, flanked by every man and his dog wanting to talk to her.

'Your grandmother is amazing,' I say as I watch her interact with her eager fans.

'She's something, alright,' he says.

I look up at him. 'You don't mind, do you? Me writing your grandfather's memoirs?'

A cloud passes over his eyes, but it is gone in a moment. 'No, I don't mind. I think you are the perfect person to write them. My grandfather really loved reading your articles.'

'I wish I'd met him,' I say.

'I wish you had too. He would've loved you.'

We stare into each other's eyes, lost in the moment, the rest of the world forgotten.

'I love you, Isobel,' he says, his voice husky. 'I've never felt like this about anyone in my life.'

'I love you too, Christian,' I say. 'So much that it scares the crap out of me.'

He pulls me close and lowers his lips to mine, kissing me gently, but possessively.

'Come home with me tonight,' he whispers against my ear.

'Yes,' I say.

CHRISTIAN LIVES in a beautiful penthouse apartment on Fifth Avenue. Double-height windows lead out onto a large balcony with a spectacular view of the city. Sparsely decorated, it looks barely lived in, but both the bar and fridge are well stocked. Christian looks at home in the kitchen as he prepares us a midnight snack and a nightcap.

'I'm not here much,' he says with a self-conscious shrug. 'Basically just to sleep, but my housekeeper makes sure the fridge is always full for the rare occasions when I have to cook for myself.'

'You cook?' I ask with a skeptical eyebrow raise.

He chuckles. 'Scrambled eggs, omelettes and cheese platters are about the extent of it.'

He places a cheese platter on the bench in front of me with a flourish. I pick up a piece of brie and let it melt on my tongue. 'Delicious,' I say, opening my eyes and looking into his.

He is the first one to break our heated stare, and he sips his drink before looking back at me.

'So...we should probably—'

'No,' I say, slipping off the stool and coming around to his side of the bench, sliding my body against his. 'There will be time enough tomorrow to talk,' I say, untying his bowtie and releasing the top button of his dress shirt. 'Tonight I think we should let our bodies do the talking.'

He cups my face in his hands, his fingers sliding into my hair, and he lowers his mouth to mine, sipping from my lips. My bones melt and I press my body against his, needing to be closer to him. My hands skim over his chest and shoulders, underneath his jacket, slipping it off his shoulders. He lets go of me enough to let the jacket fall to the floor and then his hands are back on me, under the soft chiffon cape and spanning the expanse of my naked back.

'Did I tell you how beautiful you looked tonight?' he asks. 'This low-back has been driving me crazy all night, and the slit in the side with those tantalising glimpses of the tops of your stockings? It took everything in me not to whip you away earlier.'

I take a step back from him and unzip the side of my dress letting it slither down my body leaving me in nothing but those stockings, my panties and my Louboutins.

He swears softly under his breath as his eyes roam over my nakedness. I reach up and pull the pins from my hair letting my curls fall loosely around my shoulders. His eyes darken and he removes his shirt before taking me in his arms and pressing our skin together. There is nothing like being skin on skin with Christian and I moan my approval.

He scoops me up in his arms and kisses me before carrying me out of the kitchen and into his bedroom. He lays me on his bed, removing my shoes one at a time and then taking his time as he rolls my stockings off my legs, following the path with his lips. No one has ever made me feel as sexy and wanton as Christian does. He is such a sweet gentleman in everyday life, but in the bedroom he is transformed.

He removes my panties with his teeth, his hands caressing me and then stands back to admire me. I'm not shy under his gaze, he makes me feel beautiful even though I know I'm not perfect. Those imperfections don't matter to him and the way he looks at me makes me believe in what he sees.

Without taking his eyes off me, he finishes undressing before climbing on the bed with me. He kisses me, taking his time to reacquaint himself with my mouth and our tongues tangle. I can taste the cognac of his nightcap on his tongue and his delicious aftershave fills my nose. He overwhelms my senses until there is nothing but him.

Christian is my destiny. I have never believed that such a thing existed, but just like he has opened my eyes to the other wonders of the world, he again proves my beliefs wrong. Christian and I are made for each other. Our bodies fit together in a way I didn't know was possible, and I know that there will be no one else for me.

'Izzy,' he breathes in my ear as we move together. 'My beautiful Izzy.'

I hold him tightly, arching my greedy body against his in response. I never want to let this man go. I want to hold on to him forever. I can no longer imagine what my life would look like without him in it, and I have no desire to find out. For once in my life I will fight to keep something I love.

Our bodies come together in a passionate climax that would rival a New Year's Eve fireworks display. He rolls us to the side and gathers me close to him, my back to his front, his arms wrapping around me possessively.

'Promise me you won't try to run this time,' he whispers sleepily in my ear.

'I promise,' I whisper back.

'I love you Isobel and I am going to keep reminding you everyday just how much.'

'I love you too Christian.'

He nuzzles my neck and I let my eyes full shut knowing I am exactly where I need to be.

# Day Twelve

*24th December*
*Christian's Apartment, New York City*

I don't want to move. Waking up entwined with Christian, his arms around me, our legs is some complicated Celtic knot, I have absolutely no desire to move a muscle. I just want to lie here and soak up this feeling of rightness, bask in the love of a man that has changed my world.

'You're still here,' he says, his voice gruff from sleep.

I smile. 'Where else would I be?'

'I thought last night was a dream and I would once again wake up to an empty bed.'

I roll over so I'm facing him. 'You can't get rid of me that easily,' I say, pressing a quick peck on his nose before kissing his lips.

He tightens his arms around me. 'Good, because I intend to keep you.'

He kisses me deeply and I allow myself to be carried away on the passionate journey he is taking me.

I could happily wake up like this every day. The delicious feel of Christian's naked body sliding against mine, his sweet murmurs of love in my ear, the gentle caress of his hands and his lips. What a way to start the day.

After making love, we share a shower and I'm pleased to say that his shower is just as good as the one in my hotel suite. I don't know how I'm ever going to go back to a normal shower head when I go home.

Oh. I'll be going home to my lonely little flat in inner Sydney. We still haven't worked out the logistics of our relationship... or even what to label our relationship.

'Hey, where'd you go just now?' Christian asks me, tipping my face up to his.

'Nowhere,' I smile bravely at him, pushing my errant thoughts to the back of my mind.

'You're not worried about tomorrow are you, with my family?'

I shake my head and then stop. 'Oh God. I need to buy presents!'

He laughs and pulls me into a wet embrace under the steaming water. 'Don't be ridiculous. We don't buy each other gifts. You don't need to bring anything but yourself.'

'You don't give gifts?' I ask, confused.

'Not material gifts,' he clarifies. 'We're a wealthy family; if we want something, then we can usually buy it ourselves. So instead of giving gifts, we do other things.'

'Like what?'

'Like making a donation to a charity in someone else's name or buying a goat for an African village. One year, my sister gave me a book of vouchers for different chores she would do for me.'

'You have a sister?'

'Yes, and a brother. Didn't you do your research?'

I shake my head, and he smiles fondly at me. 'I'm kind of glad you didn't Google me, I don't think we would be standing here together in my shower if you had.'

I press up on my toes and kiss his lips. 'I'm glad too, although you are pretty irresistible.'

'I am, am I?' he asks, his eyes darkening with suggestion.

'And insatiable,' I laugh as he grabs me around the waist and drags me from the shower.

'I don't hear you complaining,' he says as he tosses me onto the middle of the bed.

'Oh, I'm not complaining,' I say before he covers me with his body and kisses me.

My stomach chooses that moment to let out a loud growl, and he laughs. 'We should probably feed the beast first,' he says.

'Uh uh,' I say. 'You need to finish what you started.'

I drag him down to kiss me again, and we forget about breakfast for a while.

Later, when our baser hungers have been satisfied, my stomach reminds me it is yet to be fed. Christian jumps out of bed, pulling me up with him.

'I'm going to cook you breakfast,' he declares, and I laugh as I follow him into the kitchen. 'You sit,' he says, pointing to the stool at the bench.

I follow orders and take a seat while he moves about the kitchen with ease. He makes me a k-cup, which I sip while I watch him prepare a monster omelette. No one has ever cooked me breakfast before, not even Michael, and I feel stupidly loved by the simple act. Christian has been the catalyst for a lot of firsts in my life over the last twelve days, and I know that there will probably be more to come.

'Hey, did you upgrade my flight to first class?'

He blushes sheepishly.

'You did! Oh my God, and my room at the hotel?'

'Guilty,' he says.

I shake my head. 'You're incredible. The dress and the invitation were obviously from you too.'

He shrugs his shoulders. 'I can't help it. I enjoy doing things for you.'

I slide off the stool and walk around to hug him. 'Thank you,' I murmur against his chest.

'I NEED TO TELL YOU SOMETHING,' Christian says and I am immediately on alert. We are sitting at the table out on his balcony and have just finished eating the delicious omelettes that he made for us.

'Okay,' I say cautiously.

He sighs and sits back in his chair, his eyes going distant. 'I know that what I am about to tell you is going to put you in an awkward position, but I don't want there to be any secrets between us. I also know that by telling you this, I will be putting the fate of my family in your hands.'

I swallow thickly and sit up, leaning forward on the table. If it's something bad, I need to face it head on.

'Okay,' I say again, encouraging him to go on when he falls quiet.

'How much of the Mr Toys story have you worked out?' he asks, looking directly at me.

'Not much,' I admit. 'I'm supposed to file my article tonight, but I've got nothing new. Why?'

He looks at me as if he is trying to decide about something, and then he speaks. 'What would you say if I told you I knew who Mr Toys is?' I gasp. 'Not just know him but am intimately acquainted with him?'

'I would be... speechless.'

He shoots me a quick smile before sobering. 'You know it started in Australia, in Sydney actually.' I nod, not daring to breathe. 'After the Second World War, the economy was in a bad place and there were a lot of displaced children. Mr Toys started rounding them up on Christmas Eve and feeding as many of them as he could. The next year he did it again, but this time, he gave them each a small gift, something he'd made himself. Every year he did it again and again, reaching more and more underprivileged kids until eventually, he had a distribution centre in every state. Obviously, he couldn't get to every child who was needy, but he did what he could and reached as many as he possibly could.'

'Where did he get the toys from?' I ask.

'At first he made them himself and then, when that got too much, he employed homeless men and women to make them. Each person was given a specific toy for them to produce, and he trained them. He paid them a small wage and fed them every day that they came to the factory. Soon, even that wasn't enough to keep up with the demand. He had to create an entire company just to produce the toys, and he always employed those who needed the job the most. Some of the ones who had been working with him from the early days, he promoted to management positions.'

'How...how did he afford all that?'

'Luckily, he had a separate, substantial business that he used to finance his Mr Toys venture.' Christian chuckled. 'I don't even know who first coined the term, but he went with it, capitalised on it. Soon he was reaching out to other countries. He started small in each country and used a local workforce to build the toys.'

'It's your grandfather, isn't it?' I say, putting the pieces of the puzzle together. 'Your grandfather is Mr Toys.'

He beams a smile at me. 'He was, but it actually started with his father. My grandfather took over not long after he married my grandmother.'

'So who... oh,' I say, the last piece slotting into place. 'You're now Mr Toys.'

He nods, a proud smile splitting his face. 'My grandfather gave my uncle the choice—'

'Not your father?'

He shakes his head. 'No, my father married into the family. My mother is the eldest Hayden child, and she married my father, a Palmer.'

'Okay, so your grandfather wanted to keep it in the family.'

He nods. 'My cousins are off doing other things, but I have always been close to him, and I've known from a very young age he is Mr Toys. I even helped him out sometimes.'

'And now you're carrying on the legacy,' I say, stunned, sitting back in my chair and staring at the man across from me.

He nods sadly.

'And no one else knows?'

He shakes his head. 'There's nobody left who remembers the early days. All the workers now sign non-disclosure agreements, but none of them have ever been told the full story. Most of them think it is a corporation and not a man.'

I nod, remembering the comments I'd heard from the crowd a few days ago outside Toyland.

'Was Toyland your idea?'

He shakes his head. 'Granddad wanted to make his toys available to everyone, without diminishing the specialness... does that make sense? He still wanted to give away as many as he could to the kids that really needed a little bit of joy in their lives, but he also wanted to make his toys available to those who could afford to pay for them.'

I nod, understanding. 'I really wish I could have met your grandfather. He sounds like an exceptional man.'

'He was,' Christian says, his grief evident. He takes a deep breath. 'So, you see why I am a little worried about you writing his memoirs.'

I exhale harshly, finally realising the moral dilemma I'm facing. 'You want me to keep the secret.'

'I do.'

'I really appreciate you sharing this with me, Christian,' I say.

'I know it sounds selfish,' he says. 'But if the world knows who Mr Toys is, then it loses its... magic.'

I know he is right, but I'm a reporter, and my editor commissioned me to break the story of who Mr Toys is. Not to mention the memoirs Grace wanted me to write. Was it more important to keep this secret or to keep my integrity as a journalist?

Christian stands and comes over to me, leaning down to kiss me. 'I'll leave you to think it over. As you can probably imagine, today is going to be a busy day, what with Toyland opening and the distribution of millions of toys to be coordinated. There is a car and driver for you to use. You are welcome to stay here tonight, but I won't be home. I will, however be here to pick you up at eight o'clock in the morning to take you to my family's Christmas Day celebration.'

And then he walks away.

I AVAIL myself of the car and driver that Christian has provided for me, and I head back to the hotel, my mind full of confusion. I borrowed a t-shirt and a pair of shorts from Christian's drawers so I don't have to do the walk of shame through the hotel lobby in my evening gown.

As soon as I am ensconced in my room, I shower and dress, all the while mulling over what Christian told me this morning. I can't sit still and pace around the room when my phone rings. I answer distractedly.

'Go for Isobel,' I say.

'Isobel, it's Maryanne. Please tell me you've got a story.'

I pause in my pacing and bite my lip.

'I have a story,' I say and hear her exhalation of relief as I pace again.

'Thank God,' she says.

'What does it matter, anyway?' I ask. 'The magazine will be gone by the new year.'

'But we've got one last edition to put out there, and I'd rather go out with a bang than a whimper.'

'Are you sure this is the right story though?' I ask.

'It's the perfect story,' she says. 'What would be more fitting for a magazine called Iconoclast than to go out debunking the myth of Mr Toys? The guy is probably a pedophile anyway, and he uses this ruse as a sick way to entice kids into his house of horrors.'

'Oh, come on,' I say. 'That has got to be the lamest idea you've ever had. No way is this guy a pedophile. You've been in this business too long if you think that.'

'Maybe,' she replied and I can imagine her shrugging her shoulders. 'But I'm not the only one who is jaded because of this industry. You are not that far behind me.'

Sadly, what she says is true. Well, it was true until I met Christian.

'Look, I have to go,' I say. 'This story won't write itself.'

'Good girl. I can't wait to read it.'

I'm shaken by what Maryanne said. Was I heading in the same direction, suspecting anyone and everyone and believing that no one did a good deed without getting something in return? I didn't like that trajectory. Since being exposed to Christian's seemingly interminable optimism, I had begun to like his way of thinking. Not every good-deed-doer had nefarious purposes; some people just liked helping other people.

I grab my bag and head out, stopping in the foyer when I see my friendly bellboy.

'Hey, can I ask you something?'

'Sure,' he says with a smile.

'If you could find out who Mr Toys is, would you want to?'

He stops and thinks for a moment. 'I'd like to thank him, but part of the magic is not knowing who he is. It's nice to think that there is someone out there doing good things without the need to be recognised for them.'

'Yeah,' I say, nodding. 'I guess you're right. Um, also, do you still have that picture with you?'

'Actually, it's in my locker, why?'

'Would you mind if I take a copy of it?'

'Um...'

'I know it's a weird thing to ask, but I'm actually writing Charlie's biography, and it's such a great photo of him. I'd love to use it in the book.'

His face brightens. 'Really? Yeah, sure. I'll just go get it for you.'

I wait impatiently until he returns with the photograph.

'Thank you,' I say as he hands it over. 'I'll get it copied and leave it at the front desk for you. Oh,' I look up at him. 'I don't even know your name.'

'Billy,' he says. 'It's Billy Connors.'

I give him an impromptu hug. 'Thank you, Billy Connors. You have a Merry Christmas.'

I wave to him and head out the door to the waiting car. I hum happily as we snake through the busy Christmas Eve traffic. The driver pulls over into a narrow lane, and I jump out.

'I won't be long,' I call to him.

I enter through the big glass doors into mayhem. Toyland is alive with kids and parents and aunts and uncles and every kind of person imaginable. The place is like a zoo, but everyone seems in good spirits, and there is very little of the holiday shopping rage that is always so evident in other stores this time of year. I climb the stairs to the mezzanine level and look down at the controlled chaos with a smile on my face.

'What brings a girl like you into a place like this?' a deep voice says behind me before a warm arm wraps around my waist.

'You,' I say as I turn and give Christian a chaste kiss.

He waggles his eyebrows at me before returning my kiss with one of his own. 'My office is just down the hall—'

I whack his arm, but smile up at him. 'I'm not here for that.'

'Could I maybe persuade you?' He leans down and places a trail of soft kisses along my neck, and it's almost enough to give in.

I moan, but pull away. 'You almost had me, but I'm being strong today.'

He pouts, and I can't help kissing him again.

'Okay, so why are you here?' he asks.

'I want you to know that I heard what you had to say this morning,' I say, looking into his eyes. 'And I want you to know you can trust me.'

He searched my face. 'Does that mean—'

'I'm not going to tell you anything else. I have an article to write, and I can't wait for you to read it. What's your email address?'

He rattles it off, and I type it into my phone. 'Great. I'll email it to you when it's done.'

He pulls me in for another hug and a lingering kiss. 'I do trust you,' he murmurs. 'I wouldn't have told you if I didn't.'

'I know,' I say with one last kiss before I pull away from him and lose myself in the crowd.

# Christmas Day

ᖗᘓᕉ

He woke me with a kiss that quickly morphed into more. It was still dark, and from the brief glimpses of the bedside clock I saw, it was only two in the morning.

'Hey,' I whisper huskily when he lets me up for air. 'I didn't expect you home tonight.'

'How could I not come home after that article you wrote?'

I wriggle out from under him and sit up. 'Really? You like it?'

'I love it. It is absolutely perfect.'

'Maryanne wasn't as pleased,' I say.

'That's probably only because she didn't think of it.'

I grin up at him. 'You're probably right.'

'I am right. I'm always right.'

'Oh, really?'

'Yes.'

He pulls me down and covers my mouth with his in a deep, passionate kiss.

'You don't think Grace will mind?' I say when he lifts his head.

'I've already spoken to her, and she loves it too.'

I feel my cheeks blush. 'I really love your grandmother.'

'And she really loves you. But not as much as I do.'

'I love you more,' I say despite it being cliché and a little on the nose.

He laughs and rolls us so that I'm on top of him. 'What made you write the article about her?'

'I spent two hours with the woman, and she inspired me more than anyone else in my life ever has. The woman is incredible, and I thought it was about time other people knew it too.'

'You're incredible, Izzy.' He kisses me again, and I let myself melt into him, wondering how I ever got lucky enough to meet a man who could make me feel this way.

Christian goes on to show me just how incredible he thinks I am, and when we are both exhausted, we fall asleep in one another's arms. As Christmas mornings go, it had been the best one I'd ever experienced up to now.

MUCH LATER WHEN the sun is up, we wake and gaze dreamily into each other's eyes. Seriously, it is kind of sickening. We are in the first flush of love, and if I had been a bystander, I would have been making gagging noises. I've never felt this sappy before, but I just can't control it. So sue me, I deserve some happy.

We have a quick breakfast, just coffee and toast, and then Christian drives us out to his grandmother's estate where we are overrun by small people and big people. Everyone is so jolly, which for once doesn't annoy me. Possibly because I'm feeling quite jolly myself.

There is a feast set for brunch, and as we sit and gorge ourselves, I get to know Christian's family, some of whom I have read about but didn't know were related to him. There are surprisingly few fights and no tension whatsoever, another first for me. Just a family who enjoy each other's company. It's a delightful change for me.

After brunch, we sit around the Christmas tree for the present giving. I have to give them props for their creativity and their generosity. Everything from wells in Africa to rickshaws in India, there is even another goat. There are also some interesting chores donated, like a month's worth of home-baked cookies and a shoe-shine promise. All in all, it is fun, and I even scored a few gift certificates too. I especially like the one where I get to laze around a pool and have cocktails brought to me.

'I know you don't normally give material gifts to one another,' I say, and everyone's attention focuses on me. 'But I hope you will indulge me with this one gift.' I turn to Grace. 'I met a young man this week who had his life changed because of the generosity of this family and especially your husband. When I heard his story, I knew that this would be the perfect present for you.' I hand her a brightly wrapped gift. Tears sparkle in her eyes as she opens it.

'Oh, Isobel. It's perfect.'

Grace turns it around for the rest of the family to see. It's a copy of Billy's photo, which I had enlarged and framed. There are a round of gasps as everyone sees the picture of Charlie with a mile-wide grin on his face and his blue eyes sparkling.

THE HOUSE IS quiet for the first time today, and Christian and I are sitting out on the back porch wrapped up in a thick blanket as we watch the snow fall. It is pretty; I have to admit. But the best part is the being wrapped up with Christian bit.

'Tell me this is better than your planned vacation to Bora Bora,' he says, nuzzling my ear.

'Hmm, I suppose it's okay.'

He tickles me until I beg him to stop.

'What I mean to say is that you and Bora Bora would be pretty fantastic.'

'Mmm, you in a bikini, that I would like to see.'

We sit in silence for a while, just watching the snow, and then he shifts and clears his throat.

'Maybe we could go there on our honeymoon.'

I twist around to face him. He is holding a small box in his hand.

'I don't know whether you noticed, but I didn't give you a

Christmas present.' He flips the lid open to display a beautiful square-cut diamond. 'I love you, Isobel. You're it for me. Will you marry me?'

I look at the ring and then at him and then back at the ring.

'Seriously?' I breathe. 'You want to marry me? Even though I am a crazy person with about a million hangups and a super klutz on top of that?'

He chuckles softly. 'Those are the exact reasons I want to marry you. Please say yes, Izzy. Say you'll be my wife.'

'Yes,' I breathe, leaning in to kiss him. 'I love you, Christian Palmer, and it would be an honour to be your wife.'

His grin lights his face, and he kisses me, sealing the deal and making me the happiest woman alive.

# Frozen Eggnog Daiquiri

Serves 4

**Ingredients**
375ml Whole Milk
125ml Thick Cream
3 Cinnamon Sticks
3 Star Anise Stars
5 Cardamom Pods, bruised
1 Vanilla Pod, split and seeds scraped
1 tsp grated Nutmeg
3 Egg Yolks
2/3 cup Caster Sugar
90ml White Rum
Ice

**Method:**

1. In a medium saucepan combine milk, cream and spices and
   bring to just before boiling over medium heat. Remove
   from heat and set aside to steep.

2. Place egg yolks and sugar in a bowl and beat until pale yellow and thick.
3. Strain milk mixture into a jug, removing pods, sticks and stars from mixture.
4. Pour a little milk mixture into egg mixture while gently mixing to loosen mixture. Gradually add all of milk, stirring all the time.
5. Return combined egg and milk mixture to saucepan and gently heat until mixture reaches 75 C (160 F).
6. Remove from heat and pour into a jug and refrigerate until cold. (To make it extra thick, freeze your mixture)
7. In a blender add the cold or frozen milk mixture, add rum and ice and blend until smooth. Add more ice to reach the desired consistency. Serve in martini glasses with a sprinkle of cinnamon.

# About the Author

Emma Lea is an artist and author of over sixty romance novels. She lives on the beautiful Sunshine Coast in Queensland, Australia with her wonderful husband. She has two beautiful, grown-up sons, two amazing daughters-in-law, an adorable granddaughter and a gorgeous grandson.

She loves to read. Reading has been her escape and her safe place. Emma's earliest memories are of getting lost in a story and it is the one thing that has always brought her happiness when nothing else could. Now she writes stories and hopes that when people read them that they can find an escape, a safe place, and a little moment of happiness when they need it.

If you enjoyed reading this book, please share the love by leaving a review and telling your friends!

*To connect with Emma Lea*
www.emmaleaauthor.com

facebook.com/emmaleaauthor

instagram.com/emmaleaauthor

tiktok.com/@emmaleaauthor

# Other books by Emma Lea

This is Emma Lea's complete book library at time of publication, but more books are coming out all the time. Find out every time Emma releases a book by going to her website (www.emmaleaauthor.com) and signing up for her newsletter.

## SWEET ROMANCES

These are romantic tales without the bedroom scenes and the swearing, but that doesn't mean they're boring!

### *The Young Royals*

A Royal Engagement

Lord Darkly

A Royal Entanglement

A Royal Entrapment

A Royal Expectation

A Royal Elopement

A Royal Embarrassment

A Very Royal Christmas

A Royal Enticement

### *The Kabiero Royals*

Royal Ruse

Royal Refinement

Royal Holiday

### *Bookish Book Club Novellas*

Meeting Prince Charming

Meeting the Wizard of Oz

Meeting Santa Claus

## SWEET & SEXY ROMANCES

In my Sweet & Sexy Romances I turn up the heat with a little bit of sexy. No swearing, or very minimal swearing, and brief, tasteful and not too graphic bedroom scenes.

### *Love, Money & Shoes Series*

Walk of Shame

### *Standalone Novels*

Amnesia

### *The Trouble With Series*

(Co-Authored with Kirsty McManus)

The Trouble with Falling

The Trouble with Fame

The Trouble with Forever

## COSY ROMANCES WITH A HINT OF SPICE

What is a cosy romance with a hint of spice?

Think Pumpkin Spice Latte...Warm and sweet and delicious with just a hint of spice to tantalise.

### *All in Good Time Series*

Just a Matter of Time

That One Time

It's About Time

Over Time

In Our Own Time

## HOT & SEXY ROMANCES

Hot & Spicy Romances turn the heat way up. They contain swearing and sexy scenes and the characters get hot under the collar.

Recommended for 18+ readers

### Brisbane City Hearts (formerly TGIF)

Love to Hate You

Want to Date You

Hate to Want You

### Collins Bay Series

Last Call

The Christmas Stand-Off

### Standalone Novels

Learning to Breathe

The Wedding Pact

The Blind Date

### Romantic Suspense

Hide & Seek

## TOO HOT TO HANDLE ROMANCES

These are definitely 18+ reads and contain graphic sex scenes and high-level swearing—not for the faint of heart

### The Young Billionaires

The Billionaire Stepbrother

The Billionaire Daddy

The Billionaire Muse

The Billionaire Replacement

The Billionaire Trap

Christmas with the Billionaire

### Music & Lyrics

Rock Star

Songbird

Strings

Sticks

Symphony

## ***The Playbook Series***

In Like Flynn

Manscaping

Game Changer

Scandal

Final Notice

## ***Serendipity Trilogy***

The Wrong Girl

## ***Hope Springs***

Unbreak My Heart

Untangle My Heart

Unravel My Heart

Unwrap My Heart

## Romantasy

Romantasy books have a touch of magic to go along with the romance – Romance + Fantasy.

Some of these books are straight up fantasy...others or urban fantasy – set in the real world, but with magic.

## ***Re-Imagined Fairy Tales***

The Poisoned Princess

## ***Crescent Isle Witches***

(Writing as Avery Glass)

Witch in the City

New Witch in Town

Witch on the Run

www.ingramcontent.com/pod-product-compliance
Lightning Source LLC
Chambersburg PA
CBHW060354180626
46817CB00008B/3004